P9-DCR-997

Early Praise for *One Hundred Spaghetti Strings*:

"*One Hundred Spaghetti Strings* is so poignant and full of life and heartache, wishing and dreaming, pain and exuberance. Bravo! Steffy's voice is honest and clear, young and yet deeply tuned in; she is a real girl, right here and now, a girl readers will want to befriend."
—Amy Hest, author of the *New York Times* bestselling *Kiss Good Night*

"*One Hundred Spaghetti Strings* is 100 percent satisfying. I've just turned the last page, and I want to start right over. I loved Steffy's tale of her imperfect family members and all her efforts to turn them into a perfectly blended concoction. Her relatives might be unmanageable, but they're the ideal ingredients for a good story."
—Julie Sternberg, bestselling author of *Like Pickle Juice on a Cookie*

"To read *One Hundred Spaghetti Strings* is to laugh, sometimes cry, and always root for this middle school cook as she rewrites the recipe for family. It's a fun, funny, smart, sometimes sad, so-true, can't-put-it-down story about the power of love, forgiveness, and hope in cooking . . . and in life."
—Cathleen Davitt Bell, author of the acclaimed middle grade novel *Little Blog on the Prairie*

"Steffy made me want to cook a big bowl of pasta and sit down for dinner with my loved ones."
—Suzanne LaFleur, author of *Love, Aubrey* and *Eight Keys*

"When life gets complicated, Steffy Sandolini heads for the kitchen. Cooking has always been her safe haven (not surprising for a girl whose first words were "wire whisk"), and with a mom left brain damaged after a car accident and an absentee dad who may or may not have the skills to take care of her and her sister, Steffy is sorely in need of sanctuary. As the plucky fifth grader cooks her way through an emotional roller coaster of a year, she begins to come to terms with the messy 'kitchen sink' of a meal that is family. This joyous, heartfelt, and achingly real novel is as satisfying as a plate of Steffy's homemade gnocchi."
—Heather Vogel Frederick, author of the Mother-Daughter Book Club series

One hundred Spaghetti Strings

Jen Nails

HARPER
An Imprint of HarperCollins*Publishers*

When cooking, it is important to keep safety in mind. Children should always ask permission from an adult before cooking and should be supervised by an adult in the kitchen at all times. The publisher and author disclaim any liability from any injury that might result from the use, proper or improper, of the recipes contained in this book.

One Hundred Spaghetti Strings
Copyright © 2017 by Jen Nails
All rights reserved. Printed in the United States of America.
No part of this book may be used or reproduced in any manner whatsoever without written permission except in the case of brief quotations embodied in critical articles and reviews. For information address HarperCollins Children's Books, a division of HarperCollins Publishers, 195 Broadway, New York, NY 10007.
www.harpercollinschildrens.com

ISBN 978-0-06-242760-1 (trade bdg.)

Typography by Torborg Davern
17 18 19 20 21 CG/LSCH 10 9 8 7 6 5 4 3 2 1
❖
First Edition

For my mom, my dad, and my sister

Contents

One hundred Spaghetti Strings

Making the Place Cards for Spaghetti Dinner

My dad was coming back home. He had been gone for two years playing music in California. And before that he lived here in Greensboro, in an apartment that we were never invited to on Cumberland—at the end of Cumberland—and we only saw him about once a month if that. And before that it was kind of blurry, like when you think you have a memory of eating green Popsicles with your sister on the porch steps with no grown-up around but then you think maybe someone told you that *they* once ate green Popsicles with their sister on the porch with no grown-up around.

I decided on the pink dress that used to be Nina's but she

never even wore it—she was going through a black phase—and so I had torn off the tag with my teeth. It looked okay on me *except* 1) the chest part was itchy, and 2) it was kind of too short, and 3) I was worried about my dad coming, so there was an "except" to everything that night.

A car door slammed and the neighbors' Doberman pinschers barked and howled. Instead of going downstairs I stayed in my bedroom and grabbed Wiley, my green dog.

I heard the front door opening and Auntie Gina saying, "Hi, James," and then my dad's deep voice saying something I couldn't make out. Then a pause, and then her saying, "Come on in." I squeezed Wiley around the middle. In the two years, we had only talked to Dad on the phone one time. Christmas, when I was nine. Now I was eleven, starting fifth grade tomorrow, and I was kind of a whole new person. I was reading longer books, I could ride my bike with no hands, and I was allowed to cook and bake all by myself, turning the oven on and everything.

I tossed Wiley back onto the bed and wiped my eyes with the backs of my fingers. Dad was here. And he was staying. My fingers still had onion smell on them from when we were cutting up all the stuff for the sauce this morning, and now, wiping my cheeks, I got that burning in my eyes again.

There was a *bang bang bang* on my door.

"Steffy," my sister, Nina, said.

My face was puffy and I knew it, and I opened the door

to Nina's puffy face, and we gave each other a look where you knew the person had been crying but they didn't say anything so you didn't say anything.

"Come on," she said. She tramped down the stairs ahead of me. I wanted to stay in my room. Forever. But then I wanted to go down more than anything else in the world. I held the railing tight. The wooden steps felt extra hard under my bare feet.

Down in the kitchen, Auntie Gina and her boyfriend, Harry, sat facing us at the table. I don't know when she had time—between making dinner and now—but Auntie Gina had taken a shower, and her thick, curly brown hair was still damp. She wore her green "hangin' around" dress, as she called it, and of course all her funky bracelets. Harry was this tall Korean guy who Auntie Gina met in college and had been with her ever since. He had on my Spud Stud apron, and he winked at me when he saw me. And sitting on the other side of the table, with his back to us, was my dad.

"Girls," said Auntie Gina, "say hi and welcome to your dad."

"Hi and welcome to your dad," said Nina, crossing her arms.

"Hi," I said, waving.

"Hey," he said, turning around and standing up. He put up his hand and covered his mouth. Were his eyes kind of watering? They were a little glassy. I wondered if we should hug him, but he didn't go to hug us so I stood still, a little behind Nina. I grabbed a piece of the elastic-y material on the chest part of the dress and moved it back and forth. I peeked down and saw I was making a red mark there, but I just had to scratch.

My dad had Auntie Gina's keys in his hands.

They were his keys now. And this was his house now, and we were supposed to be his daughters. Having him there holding those keys and then seeing all the suitcases and bags and backpacks and plastic sacks by the front door bulging with Auntie Gina's stuff was forcing me to admit that it was all happening.

Our auntie Gina was moving out.

She had taught me to read. She got me cooking and baking. She had stayed awake with me when I was scared.

Taking his hand from his face, my dad said, "You've both gotten so tall." He shook his head. "My girls."

Nina said, "Ha."

Yeah, we are your girls, I wanted to say. *We've always been.*

"Nina, look at you," he said. Yeah, everyone looked at Nina, always. Boys in the grocery store turned around to get a second look. Sometimes older guys, too. This always made Auntie Gina put her arm around Nina and walk faster. Even the person in the car next to us would do a double take. Nina was an I-don't-even-wear-that-much-makeup girl. Dark-blue eyes and a wide smile and thick, dirty-blond hair.

But she didn't care that she was pretty, and she didn't act like she wanted everyone to notice her.

Wow, I thought as I looked at them looking at each other. A mirror. She'd be as tall as our dad, maybe, in a few years. They had the same hair. And a little swagger—this kind of swaying thing like they both heard their own music and kind of moved along to it.

"And Steffy," he said. "Little Steffy." There was something in his eyes that drew me right in, and I could have sat right down and told him and asked him everything. *Why are you here, will you stay, do you love me, what do you want me to be, do you remember tickling us on the green chair?*

Instead, Nina said, "This is fun."

"Well, James," said Harry, Auntie Gina's boyfriend, pushing back his chair and standing up, "come on up and we'll get you settled."

While Harry picked up our dad's duffel bag and briefcase and walked him upstairs to Auntie Gina's room (his new room), I set out the place cards I had made last night. All the drawings I'd done on them seemed babyish and stupid right then, but Auntie Gina made me put them out anyway. It had felt weird writing the word *Dad* on a place card, like he was a character in a play or something. Not a real person. I put "Dad" across from me and Nina, and Harry and Gina at the heads of the table.

"So, this is, like, really happening?" Nina asked as she set the bowl of tomato sauce on the table.

Auntie Gina laid down the knife she was using to slice the garlic bread and said in a whisper, "Nina, he's the only daddy you've got. Plus, he's got rights I don't have. It's time you girls had him back."

"No," said Nina, "it's time us girls had a choice in the matter. Right, Steffy?"

"I don't know," I said. I didn't. Nobody had ever really said that we could choose what we wanted to have happen to us.

We put down the rest of the dinner stuff, and the smell of the sauce that had been simmering since sunrise calmed me down. When we made Italian food, this house seemed more like home than ever. It had always been my mom's specialty. But I couldn't imagine eating anything. My stomach felt like it was full of bedsprings and someone was jumping on that bed.

Auntie Gina had lived with us since my mom's accident when I was three. It was another foggy memory where Grandpa Falcon (my dad's dad) came into the living room while Nina and I were eating apple slices with the peeling off and watching *Dora*, and he said our mom got hurt in the car accident and that she was in the hospital. He didn't turn off the TV while he told us, and when he finished, we kept watching. Since then our mom's lived at the Place and gets taken care of by her nurse, Helen. I don't really remember her anywhere but there.

Dinner with everyone was like watching a movie. I didn't feel like I was really part of it. All I know is I kept pulling the elastic on my dress back and forth across my chest, digging into the itch. There were a lot of fork clinks and chewing and swallowing noises. Harry told Dad a story about taking his car to the mechanic. I didn't have anything to say about getting your oil changed, so I could kind of just be in my own head, sneaking looks at my dad.

Noticing his long fingers around the fork, his mouth when he chewed. Feelings all jumbling around inside of me. I wished I were chopping the onion for the sauce right then, like I did this morning, so there would be an excuse for me wiping my nose all the time. Then Auntie Gina was saying things to bring me back to the table.

"So, the girls'll ride their bikes to school after you get your bus to work," she said to Dad. "And Nina has dance after school on Mondays, Tuesdays, and Thursdays—it's a confusing schedule—and Stef comes home alone on her bike."

Auntie Gina nodded at me. "Also, you'll need plenty of groceries in the house," she said. "We've got a budding Julia Child on our hands here. I guess the two of you can take the bus to the Harris Teeter each week, James. . . ."

I glanced shyly at my dad, who was spooning sauce onto his second helping of pasta. I wondered what sitting on the bus next to him would be like. I wondered what we'd talk about. I hoped I'd be able to think of something to say.

I managed some sweet tea and a few bites of spaghetti and one meatball. I had helped roll out the dough and turn the crank on the pasta maker, catching the noodles as they slid down my palm.

After everyone finished eating, I helped Auntie Gina put dishes in the dishwasher, and she made Nina go load sacks and backpacks into Harry's car. My dad and Harry sat in the living room talking about man things. Harry could talk to anyone about anything. He was always asking people about themselves and then bringing up more things about what they said. He reminded me of the big, green easy chair that used to be at my Grandpa Falcon's—worn in and comfy, and it would always hold you. Maybe my dad would end up being something like that.

After Harry had gone home and my dad was up in his new room, I went and changed out of the dress and into my pajamas. It didn't feel right that he was in that room two doors away. It didn't feel right that Auntie Gina was setting up a blanket on the couch. She'd sleep over that night to help get everyone settled, but nothing felt settled at all.

My whole chest was burned with all the scratching, and the coolness of a big Greensboro Grasshoppers T-shirt was a relief. I went downstairs to say good night to Auntie Gina again. Her and Nina were on the couch, and when they saw me, they stopped talking. Auntie Gina leaned in and kissed Nina's cheek, and then my sister hurried up the stairs, her arms crossed in front of her.

Auntie Gina and I were quiet. There wasn't really anything more to say about it. We stood up for a big hug, and I breathed in her pear lotion.

"I love you, Steffany. And I know you're going to be just fine," she whispered. Her silver bracelets clanged together as she grabbed me closer.

I didn't feel just fine. I felt like that long, wide piece of dough traveling through the pasta maker, coming out a hundred spaghettis. Before this night, there was Auntie Gina, always asking us if we did our homework, always letting me make messes in the kitchen, always there to pick up Nina from dance. Before this night, it was all Auntie Gina. Now she was leaving, our dad was staying, and I felt like I would never be whole again.

Chocolate Chip Banana Bread on the Flower Wreath Plate

There were tons of handwritten and newspaper-torn-out recipes spilling from my mom's old *Better Homes and Gardens* cookbook, and the banana bread one was stained with cooking oil and felt like cloth between my fingers. Each of her recipes always got me imagining her writing down the ingredients and wondering why she liked it, where she got it, when was the first time she made it. Auntie Gina might know or, if not, the answers were stuck somewhere in my mom.

While I mixed the wet ingredients (eggs) with the dry ingredients (flour, salt, and baking soda), I thought about how I was half Sandolini (my mom's side) and half Falcon (my dad's). How it was like me and Nina were the eggs and Dad was the flour. How Auntie Gina had just dumped us all into the bowl together without mixing us up with her wooden spoon.

When Dad left for California, Nina started saying her name was Nina Sandolini instead of Nina Falcon. Auntie Gina didn't say she couldn't. And then I started doing it, too. I liked having an "S" first name and an "S" last name. Pretty soon teachers started calling us Sandolinis instead of Falcons. I always wondered if they talked to Auntie Gina about it, but I never asked. Now that Dad was back, I hoped he wouldn't be mad that his last name was missing from my signature.

I had everything ready for him for when he came down. His piece of banana bread was on one of the nice plates with flower wreaths, and my piece was on a paper plate.

Dad said, "Hey," and I said, "Hey." He poured himself a cup of coffee and then said he was going outside to get the newspaper. I sat perfectly still, maybe I didn't even breathe. I hoped he'd like his breakfast. When he got back in with the paper, he sat down in the chair that didn't have banana bread in front of it. I reached across the table and slid the plate in front of him.

"Oh, no thanks," he said, opening the paper. "I'm not a big breakfast guy."

The pictures in my head of him loving the moist, fresh-baked bread, and of me showing him Mom's old recipe, and then him telling me about a time she made this banana bread for him—those pictures went away, and I wanted to go get under my covers with Wiley. It felt really dumb to eat banana bread by myself. But it smelled so good that I did anyway.

Nina came down in a black tank top and purple shorts. She took one of her earphones out and a song with maracas and drums blasted from it.

She said, "I need a new combination lock for my bike."

"I can bring you one tonight," said Dad.

"Can't you just give me money and I'll get one after school?"

He reached into his pocket and came out with a folded wad of money. He put five dollars on the table in front of her and five dollars in front of me. "Go to Hal's on Huntington," he said. "He won't rip you off."

I could tell Nina wasn't expecting him to just up and give her money. I could tell she was trying to pick a fight. "Um, Dad, Hal got sick and closed that place like two years ago."

"Really," said Dad.

"Yeah. So, like, what's your job exactly?" she asked.

"Painting an apartment complex."

"Sounds stimulating," she said.

Dad put down his mug. "I wouldn't call it that, but I'd call it work."

"New for you, huh, Dad?"

"What?"

"Work."

"All right, Nina, let's get started off on the right foot."

"I'm on the right foot, Dad. I'm always on the right foot. So, like, you came back here to paint an apartment complex?"

"I came back home, Nina, is all. All right? I just needed to come back home."

She slapped her hand on the money and slid it off the table. Then she reached over, snatched Dad's banana bread, and headed upstairs. "This looks awesome, Steffy, thank you," she said. In a minute her bedroom door slammed. The whole time, the newspaper stayed up in Dad's face. I coughed because it was so quiet with us just sitting there.

He got up and put his mug in the sink. I wondered if he was noticing the picture of Mom, her high school senior picture that Auntie Gina had hung up a long time ago next to the window above the kitchen sink. She's in a tank top dress, and her wavy brown hair is all down at her shoulders, like mine, and her brown eyes are shining at the camera, and her mouth is open in a smile like she just heard something funny. If my dad was noticing, he wasn't saying anything.

I thanked him for the five dollars. He told me to have a great first day of fifth grade, and I said I would. He called up, "Bye, Nina," and she yelled down, "Bye." He told me to remember to lock the door behind me and then he was gone. We had never done this—the thing where the grown-up leaves first. I wondered what box Auntie Gina was unpacking over at Harry's right then.

Since there was basically the whole loaf of banana bread left, I made a couple peanut butter on banana bread sandwiches for my and Nina's lunches. When they were packed up and dishes were in the sink, I ran up and put my five dollars in my ice cream sundae bank. I tucked in Wiley and put a book next to him: *Everything on a Waffle* by Polly Horvath, one of my very, very favorites.

Nina burst into my room and threw something on my bed, then disappeared, closing the door behind her. There on my unicorn sheets were three bras. A purple one, a white one, and a light-blue one. Only the white one had been worn, because the other two had tags on them. I remembered when Auntie Gina had made Nina get these—once when we were getting new shoes in Dillard's when I was in third grade and Nina was in sixth.

"Hurry," she called from the hallway. "I'm not being late on my first day of eighth grade. I've been waiting to rule the school since kindergarten." The floor rumbled as she pounded down the stairs in her big black boots.

I pulled off my T-shirt. It took a couple tries getting on the white bra, but I finally managed to clasp it together in back. Now that I had it on, I got this great panic that I might not really need it after all and that people at school would look at me and see it through my shirt and laugh. But the pink dress hanging in my closet made me think that, yes, I needed it. Yes, it was time.

I tramped down the stairs and met Nina in the kitchen, and we locked the door behind us. Right as we were getting on our bikes, she got a call on her cell from Auntie Gina wishing us a happy first day of school. My eyes welled up and Nina rolled hers, and everything that morning was just happening too fast.

As we pedaled down Buckingham Road, I thought about how Dad didn't really know us yet. How he had to get to know us because, if he didn't, maybe he would get bored and maybe he would go back to California. And then, with Auntie Gina all moved into Harry's house, I didn't know what would happen to me and Nina.

But our dad was home now, and he would get to know us. And like us. He would eat my breakfasts, and he would see the way that Nina looked out for me. And he would like that. And he would stay.

Greasy Spoon

I knew California had all those fancy beaches and famous people, but I couldn't see why anyone would want to leave Greensboro. By summer's end, the crepe myrtles and magnolias were all overgrown, and their petals littered the sidewalks like when meat is so tender it falls right off the bones. I remember at Grandpa Falcon's barbecues, he'd do barbecued pork chops and beef ribs and chicken legs. And I remember how, when you picked up a drumstick, hunks of juicy meat would slide right off the leg bone. For me, it's all about the cooking down here. Yam-pecan pies, Brussels sprouts and egg whites, chicken and waffles. I didn't know what kind of foods they cooked in California—I guessed fish because it was next to the ocean—but my dad was born here in North Carolina, and I was hoping that he still liked that Southern cooking.

The bike ride to the Greensboro Four school only took about ten minutes, and when we got there, me and Nina headed right into the gym for the first community meeting of the year.

Greensboro Four was a private school, and we had both gone there since kindergarten. Every summer Auntie Gina had to fill out the State Grant for Family in Crisis paper. She had to show how our mom still lived at the Place and how our dad was kind of not really being our dad. She would sign her name where it said "guardian," and then the state of North Carolina would pay our tuition. I started noticing these papers the summer before third grade, when our dad had just moved to California.

On the paper this year, Auntie Gina said that our mom was still at the Place but that our dad was coming back. Thank goodness our tuition still got paid for. All my friends were here at this school. And with Dad's shaving cream smell in our house, Auntie Gina's stuff all gone, and me with those new straps under my shirt, I liked coming back to Greensboro Four, where I recognized everything.

Once everyone was all seated with their grades, Principal Schmitz-Brady welcomed us back to school.

"Our campus is not simply a school, it is an education

celebration, a breeding ground for risk taking, for standing up against adversity, and for realizing our full potential."

Me and my best friend, Lisa Rudder, made faces at each other through this speech.

Like she did at the beginning of every school year, Principal Schmitz-Brady talked about the courage of the Greensboro Four.

Our school was named for these four black college students who sat at the Woolworth's white-persons-only lunch counter in 1960. After six months of more black people coming in and sitting at the counter, Woolworth's officially opened up their lunch counter to everyone, not just whites.

There was a book in the school library all about it that every second-grade class read that showed black-and-white pictures of the lunch counter—of guys in chef hats frying French fries, flipping burgers, and putting cheese on top of what looked like tuna melts. I didn't know why I remembered those pictures, but I always did. Auntie Gina would call a place like that a greasy spoon, like Your House over on Battleground. You can see the guys cooking the food right there from your table and it usually smells like bacon.

While our principal talked more, I was thinking how I couldn't wait to get to the library. The cooking section was only half a shelf long, but I liked looking at the books anyway, even though I'd read them all before. As far back as I could remember being at this school, I'd be checking out *The*

Spatula Cookbook or *Feast for 10* while other kids were checking out Dr. Seuss or *Magic Tree House*.

I was definitely in and out of Principal Schmitz-Brady's speech about bravery because I was thinking about books and tuna melts. I knew she was talking about big, important history, and I liked what my school stood for, but I was just picturing myself behind that counter frying those burgers.

"Imagine how you would have felt," she said, "if you were hungry and you were forbidden to sit down and share a meal with others."

She went on for a little bit longer and then she dismissed us to our advisory classrooms. While me and Lisa walked out of the gym together, Lisa went to put her arm around me and accidentally felt the strap underneath my shirt. Her eyes got big behind her purple glasses, and she opened her mouth in an O shape. She took my hand and reached it around to her back, and I felt the strap underneath *her* shirt.

We took each other's hand and squeezed.

"I don't know if I really need it," I said. She brought me right in front of her, held my arms out to the sides, looked down, and said, "Yes, you do. I'm the one who doesn't really need it. But who cares. I wanted to wear one anyway, to get practice."

We got to our two advisories that were right next to each other. They usually don't put best friends in the same advisory group.

Before going in, Lisa said, "So, how is it with your dad?"

"Weird."

"Has he said anything?"

"Just normal stuff. 'Hi.' 'Bye.' That kind of stuff. I can't think of anything to say to him."

"Well," she said, "eventually you'll think of something. Or at least you know Nina will."

Yeah, maybe Nina didn't always say the nicest thing, but at least she said *some*thing.

After advisory came math, my favorite. Even though Mr. Richmond was older than math itself, he always made it fun. Then science and social studies. All the teachers just said welcome, and we did overviews of the year or played games. Then lunch. Everybody was pretty jealous of my sandwich.

"What, pray tell, do we have here?" asked this boy Joe Glorioso. He'd been in our class since kindergarten.

"Peanut butter on banana bread," I said.

He lowered his head to the sandwich and took a big breath. "It smells like a divine creation from the kitchen of a celebrity chef." Me and Lisa couldn't stop giggling.

Principal Schmitz-Brady happened to be hanging around the cafeteria right then and walked over to us.

"Ms. Sandolini, may I ask what we have for lunch today?"

I told her.

"You are headed for the Food Network, my dear," she said as she trotted off to another table.

Last period was English. Lisa's favorite. My least favorite. Mrs. Ashton talked all about this huge project due at the end of the year.

"It's an autobiography," she said. "In two parts."

Some people groaned. Joe Glorioso clapped twice and said, "Hear, hear! Let the woman speak." People laughed. Mrs. Ashton snapped her fingers and raised her hand. Pretty soon everyone got quiet again.

"Part one: you will express who you are in the form of a letter written to you, from you."

Lisa was nodding and smiling. Mrs. Ashton continued.

"Part two: your mom or dad or guardian will express who they think you are in the form of a letter written to you, from them."

Lisa glanced at me from across the room, and she raised her eyebrows a couple times. She loved writing assignments, but there was a panic settling into my bones. Write a letter to myself about who I am? It was so much easier to do magic squares in Mr. Richmond's class than it was for me to think about something like this.

Toward the end of the period, Mrs. Ashton gave us five minutes of journaling time to write down our first thoughts about this autobiography assignment.

"Folks," she said, "my advice all year about this autobiography will be to be honest."

In my journal I wrote down a recipe for tuna melts. Then I froze up at the thought of asking my mom or my dad to write me a letter. I had a mom and a dad, sure, but not like Lisa or normal people had a mom and a dad. Not like you were supposed to have.

Unsalted Peanuts

Sunday was our day that me and Nina and Auntie Gina went to the Place to see Mom. But this morning there was this big thing because Auntie Gina forgot she's working in the ER now on Sundays. At the last second, a new arrangement got figured out.

Nina put her cell on speaker, and it went like this:

"Why can't we just ride our bikes over there?" asked Nina.

"It's too far for you guys to go alone," said Auntie Gina.

"We ride to school by ourselves."

"Nina, your dad will walk you over to the church, and Jean Sawyer will meet you after mass and take you. And that's that."

"Why doesn't Dad just take us?"

"You know your daddy doesn't have a car."

Obviously he didn't have a car—he took the bus everywhere. What Nina wanted to know was Why doesn't Dad visit Mom? Why does Jean Sawyer have to take us?

Well, fine. With Auntie Gina, sometimes that was just that. Dad walked us the six blocks to St. Theresa's. There was this second when we didn't know if he was actually staying for church or if he was just leaving us off—turned out he was just leaving us off. He said that he would see us later that afternoon, that Jean would drop us off at home. I didn't have to look at Nina to know that she was making a face at his back as he walked out the church doors.

After mass, Jean was waiting to take us to Mom's. "My Steffy and my Nina!" she said, grabbing us both in a big hug.

"Jean!" me and Nina said at the same time.

"My gosh, will you girls stop growing already? Nina, you're gonna tower over me any minute."

We always loved seeing Jean. Everyone did. She was always carrying bags of something interesting—fresh flowers or warm muffins. She basically did everything at church: gave out Communion, Doughnut Sundays, the carnivals and book fairs, barbecues.

We had known her our whole lives. Right after our mom's accident, we went to go live with Jean and her mom and dad for a while. Those memories for me are fuzzy, but there are pictures somewhere of me and Nina riding on her back in her living room when we were really little.

Because she sometimes had to go into the hospital, you loved her even more because you knew she didn't feel good sometimes, and you hoped she was okay. But she always got to come out of the hospital and live at home, and she wasn't like Mom at the Place. She was an extra grown-up in my life who knew I loved cooking and remembered what books I liked to read.

Today she seemed like she was feeling perfect, hugging us both hard and smelling like cinnamon. She hummed to the radio in the car, while me and Nina ate her fresh-baked scones, and going with her and not Auntie Gina turned out to be fine. Jean walked us into the Place and said she would be waiting for us in the lobby when we were ready to go.

I followed Nina down hallway D and then into the rec room. Mom sat at the piano in the corner. She had the same smile for us that she had for anyone who came.

"It's your girls," said Helen, her nurse, who was probably older than salt. Mom jumped up from the piano bench and gave us big hugs.

"Hi," she said. We kissed and hugged her back. There was that hospital smell: the generic soap from the bathrooms, the medicine-y breath. I wondered what Mom smelled like before the accident. Did she wear perfume or pear lotion? How did she fix her hair?

"Let me play a little for you," Mom said. "I've been practicing."

Helen sat back down with us on the couch across from the piano.

"Listen to 'Let There Be Peace on Earth,'" Mom said.

She leaned forward and put her finger on the sheet music and then looked down and put her hands on the keys and started. Mom wasn't the best piano player in the world. There were lots of wrong notes that made you make a face without meaning to. It's mean, but I would have maybe been embarrassed by her. But the only other resident around right then was snoring on the other couch with his legs open. Nina texted a little bit behind the piano bench while Mom performed for us.

We clapped when she finished. "You finally got that last part, didn't cha?" Helen said. Mom nodded, and Helen hugged her and rubbed her hands.

"Good for you, Mom," I said.

"I liked it." Nina came around and hugged her and kissed her cheek.

Auntie Gina had made up her mind that everyone who came in and talked to Mom could say only good and nice things to her. We could only be hugging her and kissing her and telling her she was doing such a good job at everything she tried to do. She'd said that when she visited Mom when she was in a coma, she would make the doctors who were in there not talk in front of Mom about bad things that *could* happen. She always says that we should have seen her right after she woke up from the coma—she couldn't even go to the bathroom by herself *let alone* find the words to tell someone that she even had to go at all. Now Mom was playing the piano. Auntie Gina would tell you that it's because people said the right things in her presence.

But still, she had a TBI (officially, a traumatic brain injury) and had to be introduced to us every time we came. We still had to tell her things about ourselves. I knew it was bad, but sometimes I just didn't feel like every time we met telling her how much I loved cooking. I just wanted her to know it forever.

Helen brought out the snack tray. We always braced ourselves for the hoards derves at the Place. I know it's really spelled "hors d'oeuvres" from looking in my mom's *Better Homes and Gardens* cookbook, but me and Nina called them "hoards derves." That's what I'd say when we'd play fancy party when we were little. Nina would put on one of Auntie Gina's dresses and high heels, and I'd serve pimento cheese and bologna on crackers.

I always felt guilty eating the hard candies and stale popcorn and unsalted peanuts that the nurses brought out. A taste of the bland, everyday life there. I wished I could plop our whole kitchen into this place and make pasta for all the residents one day. Or I wished Mom could come home with us for dinner sometime. But really, I couldn't imagine seeing her anywhere but here.

There was this little hint of an idea that was happening in me on that day, something with food and Mom—how basically all I had of her was her cookbook, how she was kind of just as much a stranger to me as Dad was, really, even though I saw her every week. There was just too much else happening to make me fully know what to do with this idea yet, but it was there, hinting at me.

At the Place, I always felt ashamed about this, but after a while it got boring. Maybe it wasn't boredom but just too much longing for a miracle. They said that brain injuries were mysterious, and all victims recovered differently. So maybe she'd get back to normal someday, or maybe she wouldn't.

I liked that she could play the piano and knit and do all that, but it would have been good if she asked me about a thing I'd said the last time we saw her. Like, how was the first day of fifth grade? How did the spaghetti turn out?

It would have been good if she could do some deducing, like in math, and figure things out: If Auntie Gina wasn't with us, who had dropped us off? Why?

It would have been good if she could have asked, "How do you like living with your dad?"

Brussels Sprouts and Egg Whites for Din-Din

Grandpa Falcon used to make Brussels sprouts and egg whites for dinner all the time. While we ate, the chickens in his slanting, homemade coops would bawk their heads off from the front yard. Auntie Gina loved this meal, but she'd say it was for hayseeds, that it was our duty as Italians to teach these Southerners to really *mangia*. But even though I was half Italian, I was also a hayseed, because I was born in Greensboro, just like Grandpa Falcon and my dad were.

After I turned off the eggs and popped bread into the toaster, I tiptoed upstairs with an idea. Dad would be home soon from work, but for now, it was just me and Nina, who was texting on the couch.

In the back bedroom, his fat, zipped-up duffel bag was on the floor. The bedspread was rumpled, but the bed was not even actually gotten into. Out in the bathroom it was all me and Nina's stuff: toothbrushes, toothpaste, a hairbrush, the lavender soap Auntie Gina got us. Floss. Hair stuff in the little green thing. A big bottle of Nina's new face cream stood in place of Auntie Gina's old makeup in the medicine cabinet, and of course all Auntie Gina's everyday things were gone with her. There was no man stuff anywhere. You'd think at least a toothbrush. It kinda felt like he was just visiting.

From upstairs, I heard the sound of the screen door creaking, then the front door, then the keys in the dish. I hurried down to butter the toast, fry up some potatoes, and make coffee.

Dad and I devoured our meals. Nina sat and picked at hers. It went like this:

"Steffany," said Dad.

"Yeah?"

"How did you make this so perfectly?"

I just shrugged.

"Grandpa Falcon's favorite dish," he said. "I haven't had this in ten years. Reminds me of . . . sitting at that orange table," he said, "with my dad." He closed his eyes while he chewed. "Thanks."

It was like I was playing that game Red Light, Green

Light, and I was walking forward during a green light to Dad so, so fast and I never wanted it to turn red. I wanted him to keep talking about sitting at the orange table. I wanted him to say how eating together might be making him remember a long time ago, when it was me and Nina and him and Mom.

Nina picked some more and then went over and opened the fridge and took out the peanut butter. Auntie Gina would have made her eat what was for dinner. Dad just watched her spread peanut butter onto a piece of bread and then fold it over. Auntie Gina would have said she spent time making dinner for a reason. Dad just helped himself to more.

I knew Nina remembered Grandpa Falcon reading Richard Scarry books to us outside on the yellow blanket. Cutting out paper dolls and always making this special dress he called an "orange slice" dress. Playing hide-and-seek in his basement around all those spools of coily wires and boxes and pieces of wood. How we would plug our noses because of the rotten-grape smell coming from the bottles under the stairs. I knew she remembered how we'd always get dropped off over there because Mom and Dad were gone. Those were memories that I knew for sure were real, not the foggy kind that crept up sometimes. I wanted Nina to eat with us and say something about those times, with Grandpa Falcon and Dad and maybe even Mom. I knew she remembered all those things, but she acted like she didn't.

Spooky Jell-O

It had been a month. We were getting our homework done, Nina was getting picked up from dance fine, and me and Nina were taking the bus to the Harris Teeter on Fridays after school for groceries. Dad would leave us money and had said for us to just go ahead without him. We were getting the key thing and the leaving-after-Dad-in-the-morning thing down pat. Life without Auntie Gina was scary at night, though, when it got quiet and when there was time to remember how she was in a new house across town and not two bedrooms away. The possibility of walking into her room in the dark if I needed something was gone. There was a big hole in me at night, and I couldn't figure out how to fill it up again. Dad was in that room now, and I just couldn't imagine myself talking to him if I was scared about something. Yet.

In the mornings, there was starting to be sort of a routine of him getting the paper from the porch and reading it while I made breakfast. I could get used to filling his quiet page turning by whisking eggs or mixing pancake batter. Sometimes he ate what I had made, sometimes not. When he did eat, he was more of an eggs guy than a pancakes guy. Mornings with Dad were different from Auntie Gina's chatting about her hours at the hospital or checking that I finished my fraction sheet or making Nina go wash off the black eyeliner. Different, but kind of okay.

I was keeping a list of Dad's favorite foods:

Brussels sprouts and eggs whites
anything meaty like hamburgers, pork chops, and chicken
pasta
candy (a few times I noticed a Snickers in his chest pocket).

On the first Friday in October, Mrs. Ashton asked us to take out our journals to work on our autobiographies.

"Think about this, folks," she said. "Who are you in school? Who are you at home? Are there different facets of who you are? And remember," she said, "just be honest. Now write."

I opened up my notebook to the tuna melts recipe from the first day of school and just looked around the room for a while. I could feel myself getting anxious about this assignment. At least May was a long way away, and it was only October. On her classroom windows, Mrs. Ashton had stuck those gummy-like decorations that were the shapes of fall leaves and pumpkins and bats. They looked like gummy candy. Or Jell-O.

Below the tuna melts recipe I wrote the word *Jell-O.* I wrote down some ideas for Halloween treats you could do with Jell-O, and then time was up.

Lisa came over after school. We plopped down our backpacks, and I got us some sweet tea.

"Are you hungry?" I asked.

"What do you think?" she said.

"We are so making lunch counter tuna melts," I said.

"What's the difference between lunch counter tuna melts and just tuna melts?" she asked.

"Lunch counter tuna melts are Greensboro Four tuna melts." I said. "I made them up." I explained how I remembered the book from the school library and told her about my tuna melts recipe.

"Steffy," she said, "you're funny. You would remember that book. But you better start writing actual notes on the autobiography. You're gonna get seriously behind."

"Nah," I said, licking tuna and mayo off the spoon. I just didn't want to think about it. "Can you hand me the cheese?"

"Yeah," she said. "What did you write about today?"

I told her about Spooky Jell-O.

"We are so making Spooky Jell-O after this," she said.

We split a tuna melt, and then we decided that we'd start a business where we'd make Spooky Jell-O and other unique holiday desserts and donate them to places like where Mom lives. Lisa said it'd be hard to actually make money if we were donating and all. Yeah, maybe we could sell some to schools for school parties and donate the rest.

First we mixed up a thing of orange Jell-O like it said to do on the box. Then we put it in the fridge for a while to solidify before dumping in a bunch of gummy spiders and worms. We put it back in the fridge to chill and went up to my room.

Lisa stood in front of my bed and spread her arms out wide.

"I'm being a supernova this year," she said. "I'm doing both my arms in tinfoil and then wearing this silvery leotard and these pants my mom's making that actually light up."

"Oh my gosh, that's perfect," I said."You have to use your lunar-talkies somehow, too."

"Absolutely," she said. Last year for her science fair project she had made this whole cockpit of a rocket ship thing and had gotten these walkie-talkies to show how astronauts communicate with Earth while they're in space.

"You're going to the moon someday, Lisa Rudder."

"I hope so," she said, collapsing next to me on the bed. "But you know what? You have to have 20/20 vision."

I shrugged. "You'll get contacts. That's all."

"But I like my glasses," she said, sliding them to the middle of her nose and making a funny face at me. "What are you being?" she asked.

"A jar of peanut butter."

"How!"

"Decorate a poster board and curve it around me."

"Genius."

Later we slurped down almost all the Spooky Jell-O at the kitchen table. So much for selling or donating that batch. There was only a small blop left over when Dad got home, carrying his briefcase thing. I offered it to him, and he said no thanks. Then he went upstairs and closed his door. So I left the rest for Nina. But she said the Spooky Jell-O looked gross. After she'd gone up to her room, the jiggly stuff and I just stared at each other.

When Auntie Gina got home on nights when I'd made something new, we'd sit together and she'd try it and she'd give me tips. Too salty (my sweet potato fries). Too much cocoa powder, not enough sugar (homemade icing). Just right (not that many things, but she did love the deviled eggs

I made once—just the right amount of paprika sprinkled on top). Auntie Gina was only across town, but it felt kind of like she was across the world.

Dad wasn't ever going to be able to tell me how much sugar to put in chocolate chip cookie dough or exactly how much hamburger meat to put in the meatball mixture. I couldn't imagine him sitting with me and Nina on the couch with a bowl of popcorn with Nina asking about shaving her legs and me wondering about making caramel corn.

He wasn't ever going to be able to do the things that Auntie Gina did. Or talk to us like that. But I wanted so much for him to talk to me at all. About anything. I wanted him to like me enough to tell me.

Marinating Chicken in an Eggy-Looking Sauce

It was a big, huge house with a triangle-shaped skylight and tons of pictures. There was stuff in there that I didn't even know Auntie Gina had or wanted or liked. Colorful vases and swirly art. In the kitchen was an enormous island like on a cooking show. Fruit bowls and a kitty cat clock that's eyes moved side to side each second. Harry got her a cappuccino maker and this fizzy-water-making thing.

For some reason, Auntie Gina seemed as new to me as all her new stuff, and I couldn't look her in the eyes. She looked like a teenager almost, in a cute gray-and-pink shirt and a jean skirt, and she was even older than our mom by almost eleven years. And there was this knot in my stomach about

Harry. Why did he have to be so nice? Why did he have to say it was okay for her to plaster pictures of me and Nina all over the place?

Auntie Gina had been marinating chicken in an eggy-looking sauce, and once we got busy rolling it in the bread crumbs, I started getting more back to normal. While she made waffle batter, Harry showed us the giant backyard that I didn't know who would play in and the garage with all his old books on leaning shelves. We got to look upstairs at all the million bedrooms and closets. In the bathroom, Auntie Gina's lotion looked foreign and out of place, like when you put your stuff in the hotel bathroom. Every few summers, when Auntie Gina and Harry could take the same days off from the hospital, they would take us to Myrtle Beach for a couple days, and we'd stay in a hotel right on the shore. It made me wonder what this summer would be like with Dad.

Harry showed us their Wall of Fame, which was tons of pictures in their hallway of me and Nina mostly, and of Harry's relatives. Seeing all these pictures of me in Auntie Gina's new house made me think of how there were little pieces of me all over the place—there were the photo albums that Mom had of us at the Place, there were these pictures and the guest bedrooms here that Gina had decorated all cute for me and Nina, and then there were all my things in my own house, like Wiley and my bike and all the possibilities in my kitchen waiting to happen. How could I ever even begin to put all this together and write my autobiography letter to myself? All these pieces of me were too scattered to keep track of. Who was I at home, Mrs. Ashton wanted to know? Which home?

Nina was yawning and being kind of rude for most of the tour of the new house, and I jabbed her a small one in the ribs. Then Harry asked us if we wanted a homemade Coke, and we said sure. Homemade Coke turned out to be these packets you can add to the fizzy-water thing, and I chose cream soda and Nina chose root beer, and you wouldn't believe it that it tasted the exact same as real soda from the store.

At dinner, Nina talked about how they didn't have hip-hop at her dance studio and how much she wanted to learn it.

"At Charlotte Rep they have hip-hop," she said.

"Charlotte Rep? The summer program, right?" asked Auntie Gina.

"Yeah," said Nina. "I want to audition this year. They have scholarships."

"When are auditions?"

"Sometime in May." Nina took a sip of her tea. "Could you take me down to Charlotte? To audition?" she asked, without looking at Auntie Gina. "I know it's far, but . . ."

"Nina," said Auntie Gina. "Between me and Harry and your dad, we'll get you there. Don't worry about it."

My face was getting kind of hot because I knew I was

being too quiet and I knew Auntie Gina wouldn't let me get away with it for much longer. She nodded toward me.

"So what's up with you, girlie?" she asked. "What's been cooking?"

"Literally," said Harry.

Did you notice I'm wearing a bra? Dad's stuff isn't unpacked. I can't fall asleep at night.

"How do you get the chicken this crispy?" I asked. The meal was a mixture of the saltiest and crunchiest fried chicken and the buttermilkiest and sweetest waffles and syrup.

"Oil," Auntie Gina said. "You want your breading like this, you've got to fry it in rivers of oil."

We talked a little bit more about how Harry liked to squeeze a blop of syrup from the bottle on each bite of chicken and waffle just so he could get the exact amount of maple flavor, and everybody laughed.

Then Auntie Gina said, "Harry and I wanted to tell you guys something."

Me and Nina stopped moving. I had been chewing, but I just let the bite of waffle sit in my mouth.

"What," said Nina.

"Well," said Auntie Gina, "it's about Thanksgiving." And then suddenly Auntie Gina was crying at the table. Harry swallowed his bite, took a drink of water, and took a breath. I did, too.

"My grandma," said Harry, "is getting sick." He rubbed

his forehead. "I'm going up to New York for Thanksgiving this year so I can see her."

"And I'm going to go, too," said Auntie Gina. She was wiping and wiping her eyes with her napkin. I crossed my arms over my chest. One annoying thing about Auntie Gina: every time something kind of big was happening, she started crying. So there was no way, ever, to be angry with her. Because you always wanted to give her a hug. But I was mad at her. She had left us, after taking care of us since I was three. Eight years. And now she was telling us that she wasn't spending Thanksgiving with us?

She said she had an easy Crock-Pot turkey dinner recipe for me and Nina to do, or she'd make arrangements for us to have dinner at the Place with Mom.

"And maybe it'll be good for you two to have Thanksgiving with your daddy this year. How is he? He doing okay?" she asked. Harry passed Auntie Gina another napkin, and she blew her nose. Me and Nina looked at each other. She shrugged one shoulder and made a face.

"I don't know," Nina said. "We see him at breakfast and dinner."

I just sat there, because it felt like if I opened my mouth to talk about how Dad didn't even put his toothbrush by the sink and how Auntie Gina's stupid pear lotion was all cute and fresh in her new bathroom, I would throw up chicken and waffles.

"Well," Auntie Gina said, after looking at us with her radar vision for a minute and maybe knowing we didn't know what to say, "tell me the lowdown about school so far." And we talked about stuff this year so far, more dance stuff from Nina, my advanced math class, this polenta recipe I wanted to try. It was like normal, us three all talking at the same time.

While Harry cleaned up, we set up stuff for the ice cream sundae bar.

When we got dropped off at home, Auntie Gina had Harry wait at the curb, and she ran in with us. Dad was on the couch watching TV with his shoes on. He must have just gotten home from work. We didn't mean to be listening so hard to their conversation, but we couldn't help it. She asked how he was doing, and he said fine. She asked if his business at St. Theresa's was going okay, and he said yes, ma'am. She asked how work was, and he said fine. I don't think his hand moved from the armrest the whole time they talked.

There was a feeling that she wanted him to say something that he wasn't saying. Or just say more. *Good luck,* I wanted to tell her. This was a guy of few words. Pretty soon we were walking Auntie Gina out the door, and she kissed us both a hundred times and wiped her eyes and said she loved us.

Even though it was the same old Auntie Gina, after being in her new house I felt farther from her, melty and almost gone to nothing. And Thanksgiving without her this year would be like serving the turkey without the stuffing.

The only thing that had made me feel better at Auntie Gina's was helping her in the kitchen. When we were rolling chicken breasts in eggs and bread crumbs, and talking about cooking oil versus butter in waffle recipes, that was the best part of my night. And it always was the best part, in all my life: doing cooking stuff. And this Thanksgiving Auntie Gina wouldn't be there with me to do that. I imagined taking a marker and crossing that Thursday out of the calendar and just going from Wednesday to Friday so I wouldn't have to wish so hard that Auntie Gina and Harry had stayed.

Carrots to the Beat

Saturday it rained all day. Usually when it was stormy, Auntie Gina would open the big window in the dining room. But she was at her new house right then, probably having leftover waffles from the dinner last night. Me and Nina opened that window and stood in front of the screen and breathed in that good wet smell of cut wood and dirt. We watched *Simpsons* reruns all that afternoon while Dad just stayed in his room. All of a sudden, a trumpet started playing from up there. Nina's head popped up from the couch.

"Huh?" said Nina. We looked at each other.

"This is 'Take the "A" Train,'" she said. "We did improvised dance to this at my studio. Oh my gosh." She sat up and started kind of swinging her head back and forth. She turned the TV way down so we could hear better, but pretty soon the trumpet stopped.

"That was Dad?" I whispered.

"Unless the pillowcase knows how to play," Nina said, flopping back down and turning the TV back up. The trumpet started again a few minutes later, and Nina slid off the couch. She lunged and lifted her arms to the ceiling. Then she moved her hips, and she held her hair and swayed. She did a high kick and then lunged again, leaning forward and bobbing her head.

Nina would leap and dance around the house sometimes, but not while an actual trumpet was playing. A couple times she held out her hand for me to join her. It was definitely a kind of movable-to song, lots of notes going around and around in this nice little melody, but I shook my head and she grinned at me. I wanted to do *something*, though, so I went into the kitchen.

While I was getting out the big flowered bowl, I was feeling like the trumpet was this stranger filling up the whole house. And when we were at Auntie Gina's, I had felt like a stranger, even though Auntie Gina was there. As I put lettuce into the bowl, I wondered if anything'd ever start to feel normal again.

Then there was the secret in the fridge. I was getting out tomatoes and carrots when I saw it. Behind the tortillas and the salsa on the bottom shelf was a six-pack of beer. I closed the door and stood back from the fridge for a second. Now it felt like this was a different person's kitchen. Well, okay. Just because Auntie Gina didn't buy beer didn't mean Dad wasn't allowed to. Right?

While I added the already-cooked grilled chicken, Nina kept dancing. I didn't mean to, but I started chopping carrots on beat with the music. Maybe the only thing to do was to welcome the strangeness in, like Nina was doing.

Then the trumpet stopped. I looked up, and she was finishing turning and then she kicked up really high, came down, bowed her head, and just stood there breathing. In a minute, Dad's door clicked open, and he came down the stairs.

"Hey," he said.

"Hey," we said.

"Dad," said Nina. "You play the trumpet now. That's new." She was panting and wiping her forehead.

"Not quite," said Dad. "I'm learning the trumpet." As I shook salt and then pepper onto the salad, I pretended I wasn't watching him stroll into the kitchen. I made myself really busy pouring dressing as he swung open the fridge and bent down. After a second, he came out with a beer. He twisted the top off, held the bottle out in front of him, and pressed his lips together. Then he took a long, long drink.

I looked at Nina, and she shrugged. "How long have you

been playing?" she asked.

"Believe it or not," he said, "I played in jazz band in high school. That's where I met your mom."

Everything inside of me lit up, like turning on the Christmas tree lights for the first time after they get strung on the tree.

"She played piano, and I played trumpet. Badly." Dad laughed at himself and so we did, too. He was talking about our mom. He hadn't said the word *mom* since he got home. Maybe he'd keep talking about her. Telling us more things. Why he left. Why he came back. When he'd come with us to the Place.

"I stunk at dance when I first started," said Nina. "Especially ballet. But then I started taking jazz and modern."

Then they talked about jazz music, how it's a theme that gets repeated. How the instruments come in and out and take turns doing their version of the theme. I cut up a loaf of Italian bread and for fun made big, small, and medium pieces: all variations on the theme of bread.

The more Dad and Nina talked, the more I didn't have to worry about thinking of anything to say or that they would fight. I sprinkled a few spoonfuls of Parmesan cheese on top of the salad, and then we all sat down to dinner and Dad drank another beer. Then another beer. He told us he'd always wanted to play an instrument and did we ever feel like that? I said no, and Nina said yes.

"I guess Steffy's instruments are all in here," said Dad, gesturing toward the kitchen cabinets. I just nodded, my whole soul filling up. I thought right then that maybe I could ask Dad to write the parent-or-guardian letter for the autobiography assignment. Even though I didn't know what I'd write about myself yet, maybe he was seeing me better than I could see myself somehow?

He opened another beer. Me and Nina watched him gulp it down. There was some kind of bell that went off inside of me—like the oven buzzer—that said, "This is wrong." But he *talked* to us. And looked us in the eye. And while he opened the next bottle, he described a California night on the beach by himself.

"So it's so beautiful there by the Pacific Ocean, you feel like you're at the end of the Earth and that there's nothing else to see." His eyes were really glassy by now. He went on and on about the strength of the waves and how loud they are when they crash. "But standing there, next to all that power, you feel like the smallest person on the Earth, too, somehow. Like you don't matter."

I get it, I know what you mean. I have felt like that ever since Auntie Gina left. I don't know where to go or who to be.

After dinner, Nina insisted on loading the dishwasher. Dad sat at the table, twisting the top off the sixth beer. I got up and started bringing dishes to the sink.

"It's like, I just always knew I wanted to dance," Nina was

saying. "Like, from when I was little. And not just take lessons or be in recitals, but *dance* dance. Like be a real dancer."

"I remember," Dad said, "picking you up from ballet."

"You do?" Nina asked, her nose wrinkling. She turned off the water and came and sat down at the table with him, even though the dishes weren't done. "Really?"

"Yeah," said Dad. "You were . . . oh God, couldn't be more than two years old. Steffy wasn't born yet. You wouldn't take off the tutu."

"Really?" she said. Her eyes got big.

He nodded. "They had a recital," he said. "You played a lamb. With ears. We were in the first row. Your mom . . ." He stopped talking and leaned his head to the side. "Your mom."

Nina and Dad sat together at the table, both looking down at their hands. They had the same shoulders, and the way that their necks craned forward looked similar. I was tossing silverware into the dishwasher and it was making a clanging noise, but I stopped clanging because they stopped talking.

They were having this minute together, about Mom, this minute that I couldn't be in because it was all about before-I-was-born stuff. Pretty quick Nina got up from the table and went upstairs. Then Dad pushed his chair from the table and grabbed the beer that he hadn't finished. He and the bottle went upstairs. I didn't think a beer had ever gone up to the bedroom, ever, in the history of our house.

I filled up the sink with lime dish soap, and the kitchen felt like the kitchen again. I washed the big flowered salad bowl by hand, because I always did that, and I put the rest of the stuff in the dishwasher. I slid the dish-drying thing toward the sink so the water from the bowl that I had left to dry could go down the drain instead of on the floor. Because I always did that.

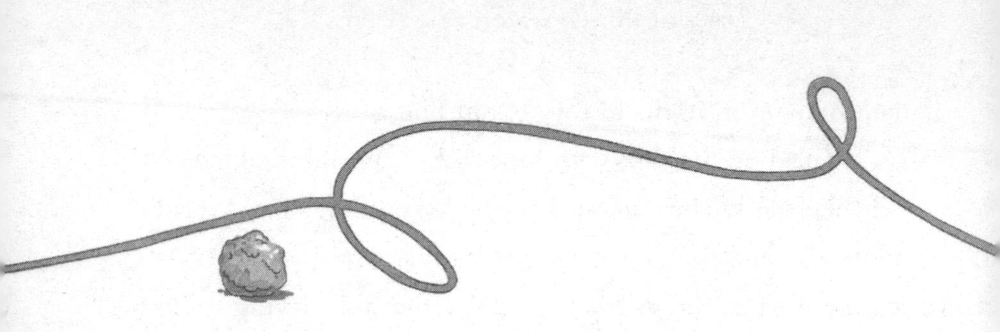

Spicy Nina-ritos

Mexican food was not my best subject—math was. But burritos were Nina's favorite, and I always liked making someone's favorite something. We cooked them for dinner before her dance concert. They really were easy: you just got a packet from the store called Taco Seasoning and dumped it into a pan with meat. I usually added a pinch of pepper to the meat, too, because everyone liked them spicy. Then you got your toppings and fillings all cut up and set them all up like a buffet so people could have fun serving themselves. I dumped tortilla chips in a bowl, too, for salsa dunking.

There was all this excitement bouncing around the

kitchen because 1) tonight Nina would dance her first solo, and 2) it was almost Thanksgiving break, and 3) it was starting to feel like a "we" in our house instead of an "us" and a "him."

"All right if I take a couple of these for my lunch tomorrow?" asked Dad.

"Sure. You can put them in your briefcase," I said.

"Briefcase?"

"That briefcase-y thing you have."

"That briefcase-y thing is a trumpet case," Dad said.

"Oh," said Nina, "yeah."

At the recital, she turned and leaped so seriously and gracefully, and there was such a sad look on her face that went with the music, I almost didn't realize it was her. Up there on the stage, she was standout good. All the girls could do the moves, but she was acting while she was dancing, and I was wishing I'd brought tissues. I thought I caught Nina looking right at Dad a couple times from the stage when she danced.

Auntie Gina and Harry had met us there, and they sat on one side of me in the theater and Dad sat on the other. This was the first time all of us went somewhere together, and there was too much in me then, with those two sides of me coming together, and I couldn't stop fidgeting with the armrest.

After the concert, we got ice cream at Uncle Louie's with

Nina's dance friend Denise and her mom. The sun had just set, and there was a breeze and a pink sky. We all sat at these little round tables outside, and I got butter pecan with caramel sauce. Everybody complimented Nina on her solo.

"Oh my gosh," she said. "I totally messed up." That was Nina. Downplaying that she had been so perfect and good in the recital. She and Denise looked like famous actresses with their stage makeup still on, and even though I was only in an orange sweater and jeans, I felt fancy just being with them.

"Steffy," Auntie Gina said, taking two sheets that she'd printed from a website out of her purse, "you can do this." It was a Crock-Pot turkey dinner recipe. I nodded. I really felt like I could. She put her hand on my hand.

"I'm gonna miss you two next week. So much." She swallowed, and her eyes watered. She licked her chocolate-and-peanut-butter scoop. A gush of cold air came out of Uncle Louie's as customers left the shop with their cones.

"This is all so hard, isn't it?" she said to me. Nina and Denise and her mom were taking a walk down the block with their cones. Harry and Dad were talking at another small table nearby.

Auntie Gina said, "Everything's so different. I don't even know how it all happened." She wiped her nose. "Just feels like yesterday me, you, and Nina were sitting on my bed setting up little towns from those little punch-out books, remember?"

"Yeah, and acting out the Point Philips family saga," I said. We laughed at the soap opera we once made up with the paper doll people. But mixed with the laughing, there was this pulling-down feeling in me. Thanksgiving was one more week away. It would be the first big holiday that I could remember that I wouldn't spend with Auntie Gina. The thing was that she had been a mom, a friend, and the funnest babysitter all wrapped into one, like a burrito with all my very favorite fillings inside. It did feel to me like our dad was getting to know us better, and even liking us, and that was so, so good. But it looked like I would never, ever get to have all those parts of Auntie Gina in my life again.

Iced Caramellatos and Bubble Tape

Greensboro Four always did a fun day of school the day before Thanksgiving. There were no classes, just activities and parties. This year fifth grade did this big thing called "Have You Ever . . . ?" where our whole fifth-grade class got into a giant circle in the gym. They turned most of the lights off, and our teachers stood in the middle of us. Me and Lisa held hands next to each other and so did other sets of friends, and everyone had a hard time calming down and getting quiet. Joe Glorioso had his hands cupped around his mouth, and while turning around in a slow circle he kept saying, "Tone it down. Tone it down. Tone it down," in a loud monotone.

Once we started the game it went like this: a teacher would read a sentence, and then if what they said was true about you, you stepped forward, into the middle of the circle.

They started out by saying things like "I have seen a movie in the last six months" and "I have listened to a song I like in the last few days." Everybody pretty much stepped forward for those. But the more the game went on, the harder it got. They said, "I have cheated on a test this year." And at first no one stepped forward, and then lots of people stepped forward. And then they said, "I have felt stressed this year." And lots of people stepped forward. Me included. They said, "I have talked to my friends about feeling stressed." I stepped forward on that one, and Lisa stepped forward, too, and we squeezed hands. I liked that we were kind of in the dark.

Then they got to saying things like "I feel like I can talk to my parents about anything." And hardly anyone stepped forward. I was glad that I wasn't the only one who hadn't. And when they said the next thing, "I feel like my parents know exactly who I am," I was glad that I wasn't the only one who stayed still. By far.

At the end of the day, everyone went to their last-period class, which for me was of course English. And of course Mrs. Ashton reminded us about the autobiography.

She said, "I noticed that during this morning's activity in the gym, you were prompted to consider whether or not you think that your parents know who you really are. I want you to write about that now."

Even though I was mad at Auntie Gina for going to New York this year, I had to admit that she knew who I was, for sure. But Dad was knowing me better now, too. Thinking about the letter, I was all torn about it. At least after playing the game this morning, though, it seemed like I wasn't the only one in my class who was having trouble with it.

Instead of writing any of that down in my notebook, I just made the list of groceries that me and Nina were getting at the Harris Teeter later. I knew them all by heart already, from the printout Auntie Gina gave me, but for some reason it felt good to write them down, too, in my own handwriting. I never liked writing very much, but maybe Mrs. Ashton was right about something: once this year she said something like "Seeing the jumbles in your head come out on a piece of paper could help you make sense of what was going on up there." Even if the jumbles were in the form of a Thanksgiving dinner list.

When we hopped off the Number 7 bus late that afternoon and headed across the street to the Harris Teeter, I was really starting to get excited about tomorrow. If I thought I might have been a little sad to come Thanksgiving shopping without Auntie Gina or if I might have wished it were Dad taking me, I turned out to be wrong. It ended up being fun with just me and Nina. Ever since the night with the trumpet, she'd been in a good mood.

Plus, it was the Harris Teeter, and besides being fun to say (Auntie Gina used to call it the Harris Tooty-toot-tooter), it's just one of the best places ever. The gush of air-conditioning when you press where it said PUSH on the front door. The perfumy smell from the bouquets up front, the scent of ground coffee from the java station. Mmmm.

Nina insisted that we stop for iced caramellatos. I'd had that *exact* thought right before she said it. We were by ourselves, after all, so no one could say no, you don't need a froofy coffee drink. Yes, we did.

We passed the guy spritzing the apples in Fruits and Vegetables and we got our potatoes. In Canned Goods we picked up the turkey stock, and in Meat we got the turkey. I guessed it was hard to pick out a good turkey because there were all these grown-ups there, lifting up turkeys and looking at them and then putting them back and getting another turkey to lift up and put back. I felt like there was a secret that I didn't know to picking out the very best one. I looked at Nina and shrugged.

"This looks good," she said, pointing. "It says 'turkey' on it, right? And it will fit in the Crock-Pot." Together we lifted one turkey into our basket.

If Auntie Gina had been with us, she would've said not to push the basket while kind of running down the dairy aisle for whipped cream, but no grown-ups were with us, so we ran. We also grabbed a carton of milk because we needed a splash for the mashed potatoes. When we got to the check-out, of course there was all that candy and gum that Auntie Gina always said no to.

"Gum?" Me and Nina looked up at each other, and both said it at the same time, and then we couldn't stop giggling for anything. We chose grape Bubble Tape. And I threw in a Snickers for Dad. We paid with the money he left us, and we got the giggles when we tried to carry all our stuff outside. Nina was managing the bag with the turkey in it plus one other bag, and I had three bags with the rest of the stuff. We were making each other laugh because we were walking all funny because it was all so heavy. There were a couple ladies from church chatting up by where you leave the baskets. You could tell they wanted to say something like "calm down, girls," but they didn't.

The bus seemed overloaded with all the grocery bag people on board, and it pulled away slowly, with everybody jabbering to each other. A big turkey bus with all the travel-ers as stuffing. Maybe for the first time since Dad moved in I was officially happy. School was out for four whole days, Dad and Nina liked each other now, and as my sister unwound just the right length of Bubble Tape for me, I was realizing that there was more than one person who really knew me in my life. That maybe I could turn in a couple letters instead of just one.

Crock-Pot Thanksgiving with the Blue-Stained Hand Guys and Cigarette Carol

Okay, this was what I did. I washed the turkey with cold water. But I dropped it, and it blanged into the side of the sink and I felt bad. Then, as per Auntie Gina's instructions, I felt around in the neck for these little gross-out bags of innards that she said *not* to cook in the turkey. Then I put the bird in the fridge overnight.

I got us up early on Thanksgiving Day. We figured out we could actually angle the TV that sits in the living room so we could watch the Macy's Thanksgiving Day parade while we worked in the kitchen. Nina put frozen waffles in the toaster, and then she helped me heft the turkey up into the Crock-Pot.

Then came Auntie Gina's stuffing recipe. You cooked the chopped onion and celery in butter, then poured that into a big bowl and mixed it with bread cubes and seasonings. We added water and tossed it like a salad. Once that was ready, I packed it inside the turkey and pressed leftover bits onto the skin, too. Then Nina poured on the turkey stock.

Santa was floating down the street in the parade when Dad came downstairs. The turkey dinner was simmering away in the Crock-Pot.

"Whoa," he said when he saw all the stuff everywhere.

"It's all Steffy," said Nina.

"Nina poured the stock," I said, wiping my forehead.

"A three-year-old could have done that," she said.

"You made waffles," I said.

"A baby could have done that," she said. "Look at you, Steffy. You're disgusting." She was talking about how my hair was all tangly and how waffle crumbs, melted butter, and turkey stock were all over my pajamas.

"Crock-Pot?" said Dad as he filled up the coffeepot with water.

"Yeah," I said. "Well, I thought that since we were gonna be at Mom's all day, the turkey would have to cook somehow."

"Yeah," said Nina. "There's always a party at Mom's," she said, "that anybody can go to who's family."

Dad's back straightened. He was facing the other direction

from us and spooning ground coffee into the coffeemaker.

"That anybody can go to who's *family*," Nina said again. She stood there a little longer, but Dad didn't turn around. I started walking upstairs to go get changed. When I was in the bathroom brushing my teeth, I could hear them talking quietly. I stopped brushing, toothpaste stinging my mouth, trying to hear what they were saying. Then Nina stomped up the stairs, flounced down the hallway past me, and slammed her bedroom door.

On the walk to church, Dad was asking me if he should do anything with the Crock-Pot while we were out, and I said to just check the turkey to make sure it reached 165 degrees inside. He said he'd have the table all set for when we got home. Nina walked on one side and Dad walked on the other, and they didn't speak. Instead of getting panicky, I was trying to notice how it was the best fall day out. You needed only a little sweater, and tree branches rocked gently from side to side. Red and brown and yellow leaves were dangling, hanging on just a little longer.

Jean Sawyer was waiting in the vestibule, and Dad said bye and I said bye and Nina didn't say anything. But then Dad did something odd. He went downstairs to the church basement. I was giving Nina lots of looks but she wasn't even letting anyone look at her, and then we were outside, following Jean to her car.

On the way to Mom's, while Jean was asking Nina what

she thought about the Broadway dancers in the parade, I couldn't stop wondering what Dad was doing in the basement. Maybe he had to go to the bathroom was all I could come up with. But there was a bathroom in the vestibule. And then I remembered what Auntie Gina had asked him after dinner at her house that night, about his business at St. Theresa's. Maybe he worked there?

We got to Mom's and headed in to the party. There were the usual decorations and food. But it was the sick-people food in a sick-people place and not *really* meant for us, even though they always invited us to get a plate. Everyone had gotten wheeled or walked outside onto the big deck where the meal was, and they sat around looking at each other and us visitors and talking slow. Some of them were actually laughing sometimes and playing Monopoly and Scrabble and Uno.

We hugged and kissed Mom, and she squeezed our hands. We drank the Place's version of sweet tea (not too sweet because some residents weren't allowed too much sugar) and went through a photo album Mom had out.

"And that's Grandpa Falcon," I said, "pig picking."

"Mmmm," said Nina. "Let me see that." We pored over pictures of this big cookout at Grandpa Falcon's. There was Grandpa, turning the spit. Grown-ups I didn't recognize holding cups of Cheerwine, it looked like. There was me in only a diaper with corn all over my face.

"There's Steffy," said Nina, "when she was the chubster." I elbowed her, and we all three giggled. It just stung, though, being close with our mom like that for a few minutes, knowing it would all go away from her by the next time we came.

When we got to her and Dad's wedding, she outlined his face with her finger and squinted. Even though I had seen those photos before, things got all disassembled inside of me when I looked at them now. Mom looked like the same mom from her senior picture that hung in our kitchen—wavy hair at her shoulders. Dad looked the same as he did now but with less wrinkles.

Somehow they looked smaller in those pictures, like they were doll versions of themselves. Nina got up with her phone after a minute. Another one of Auntie Gina's rules was that we weren't supposed to talk about Dad so much when we came. Helen gently took the album and told us Mom was playing the piano almost every day and remembering more and more of what she had practiced from the day before.

Now me and Nina sat on either side of our mom and had our arms around her and gave her kisses, and she liked that. I held her hand and squeezed, and she squeezed back. Nina handed her a plate of food, and she ate stuffing. Watching all the residents eating, I wondered if they sometimes forgot who each other were.

Jean came down hallway D and into the rec room a little before it was time for us to go.

"Hi there, sweetie," she said to Mom. "It's me, Jeannie Sawyer, your old neighbor. From Castlewood Drive?"

Mom stood and hugged Jean. "Castlewood Drive. Yes," Mom said. "There was that brick wall that we used to climb on, right?"

"Right," said Jean. "I think I fell off that wall more times than I crossed it!"

"Me too," Mom said. They both laughed hard, and it reminded me of how much me and Nina were laughing yesterday. And it got me thinking how I hardly ever heard my mom laugh. I turned toward Nina, and she looked away because her eyes were watering and she had eyeliner all over her thumbs.

When we got home, Dad and some people were out front playing cards and drinking coffee. Jean came and hugged Dad, and then he introduced us to everyone. There were three guys with dirty fingernails and blue-stained hands—just like how Dad looks when he comes home from painting all day. They were the kind of working guys who Grandpa used to give a Coke and Oreo cookies and twenty dollars to, to help repair a side of a chicken coop or go up on the roof. The kind of guys you saw sitting on the curb in front of 7-Eleven waiting for someone to ask them to paint a house. It hit me that that was the kind of guy my dad was, too.

There was also this gray-haired lady with a pack of cigarettes in her T-shirt pocket. She shook my and Nina's and

Jean's hands and said she was Carol, a friend of our daddy's.

We said "Nice to meet you" to everyone, and then Jean came in to drop off two pies she had baked for us.

"Ooooh, yummy, yummy smell," she said as she put down the pies on the counter. She was right. The turkey had been cooking all day long, and the rich smell of gravy and stuffing was so heavy in the air.

"Can you stay?" I asked her.

"Oh, hon, I have to get home to my parents," she said. "My dad's been cooking since yesterday. All the Sawyers are in town from all over."

I thanked her for the pies, and as we hugged, I silently thanked her for coming and making my mom laugh today.

Once Jean had gone and me and Nina had pretty much gotten everything on the table, we started calling the guests in. Carol came in first—she had brought two soft loaves of French bread. She even brought her own butter and little containers of garlic salt and parsley, and while people were washing up and getting settled at the table, she made fresh garlic bread in our oven. It was cozy to me when someone came over to your house and brought something to cook, and your kitchen got shared with them for that meal.

I was so nervous that all these people were going to eat what I had made, I could barely look at anyone once we were all seated. But I didn't have to be nervous. Sort of. I ended up forgetting cranberry sauce, and there was this moment when the gravy almost spilled all over Carol. But Dad caught the side of the bowl, and it only got on her jeans a little. She ended up laughing, and my heart went back to beating normally. I missed seeing the green bean casserole that Auntie Gina was famous for, but at least it was better than Charlie Brown's Thanksgiving menu. The meat had fallen off the bones, and let me tell you, it was the juiciest. Those worker guys brought store-bought apple pies, and Carol also brought sweet potatoes. Nina even remembered the whipped cream for the pies.

Everybody said, about a hundred times, how good I'd done. I kept trying to say how Nina had helped, and she kept not letting me. For some reason, I could barely talk, because my whole heart was filling up behind my face. I had never had Thanksgiving with strangers, and it was a more clinking-fork than talking dinner. But Nina put on her holiday mix, and she was talking a lot to Carol, who was really nice. It all turned out to be not that weird to eat with these people. I wondered where their families were, if they had kids somewhere. I thought of Dad in California the last two years and wondered if he ever spent a holiday with some family like us.

Kitchen Sink

It was the Monday after Thanksgiving break. Denise's mom was supposed to drop Nina off right after dance, like at five thirty. Dad was supposed to be home around the same time. On Nina's dance days, they ended up getting home within just a few minutes of each other. When it got to be six o'clock, I called her cell and got her voice mail but didn't leave a message. I called Dad's cell, and he didn't answer. What was the purpose of cell phones when people didn't answer them? Sixth grade was the magic year that you got a cell phone, in Auntie Gina's world anyway, so I guessed I'd get mine next year, and I'd answer it. I finally called the dance class place. Miss Ronnie said Nina had gone home with another girl in the class.

I didn't know if I was supposed to be worried or mad, so I just kept looking around the fridge and the cabinets for my Kitchen Sink dinner. It's where you hunted around the kitchen and threw bits of everything you had into a pot.

Even though it felt wrong to cook with nobody home, I set the table and kept going. I turned on the channel 3 news at six thirty with Bob Sebuda. I ripped off all the good leaves of lettuce and set them in a pile. Then I got rice cooking on the stove. I cut up peppers and mushrooms and fried them up together with olive oil. Then I threw in all the leftover turkey meat, too, like a substitute for chicken in a chicken stir-fry type thing. Then I poured one can of tomato sauce and one can of tomato paste over the frying veggies and meat, but it didn't smell good anymore. Quickly I added garlic powder and let it simmer.

Finally Nina answered when I called her again and said she rode home with Denise from her class and that she was spending the night and bye. She was spending the night on a school night? Who was gonna eat this dinner?

But I just kept going, because it was all cooking already, and I sort of felt like I was too late into it to stop. So I scrambled some eggs. Then I dumped the rice, the stir-fry stuff, and the eggs into a big bowl. My idea was that you could take some of the mixture and put it into a lettuce leaf and roll it up like a burrito. I sat at the table and watched the steam rise from the bowl.

I was alone but hungry. Unfortunately, Kitchen Sink was gross. I decided I had to eat it, though, so I could figure out why. I tried to give myself tips. Tomato sauce and paste: bad move. The flavor of rice and turkey on lettuce: disgusting. And overall, too much garlic powder. It was a bunch of good separate tastes, but they shouldn't have all been mixed together.

Then I turned on *Jeopardy!* and started putting stuff in the dishwasher. It was dark out. My eyes locked with my mom's eyes from the picture of her above the sink. Sometimes when I looked at that picture I liked it because she was there watching me and being with me, and sometimes I wished that picture was gone so the reminder of her being fine and okay before her accident wasn't always there, butting in. Right then it gave me a sting to meet her eyes when they were eyes from before that could have remembered everything I told her.

I called Nina's cell again, and she didn't answer. I called Auntie Gina's cell, but she was coming back from New York that night, so I knew I wouldn't get her. *I'm gonna just do everything normal,* I was telling myself. Homework. Shower. Pajamas. Teeth. The TV was blaring downstairs.

Finally, when I was getting into bed, I heard the screen door. The keys in the dish. In a second, the TV got turned down, and the fridge opened and closed. I could hear Dad getting out the bad dinner and then pressing microwave buttons. I held Wiley close to me and glanced at my clock. It said 9:36 p.m. I was wiping and wiping my eyes and nose with my sheet. I finally let myself fall asleep.

When I woke up the next morning, it felt like I hadn't moved from holding Wiley by me all night.

During dinner that night (frozen pizza, because I was scared to cook anything after Kitchen Sink), I was bracing myself for Dad to say something to Nina. Ask her why she didn't ask first to spend the night somewhere. Tell her not to do that again, like Auntie Gina would. It went like this:

"Nina, you call me if your plans change," said Dad.

Dad, you could have called me since I guess your plans changed last night, too. You never got home that late before.

"What plans?" asked Nina.

"Plans that involve who's picking you up and taking you here or there. Plans that involve letting me know where you're going and when."

"But it didn't involve you," said Nina. "You don't have a car."

"Yeah, but I'm your dad."

"But you don't have a car, and it involved cars."

"Nina, just tell me what you're up to, you hear?"

"You wouldn't've answered your phone anyway, Dad," she muttered.

And that was it. Dad ate another piece of pizza, and Nina finished her sweet tea. After dinner we all spread out: me to the sink, Nina to her room, Dad to the TV. He didn't even get mad at her. Nothing. I knew it wasn't my job to be angry at Nina for what she did, but it was someone's. I did the dishes where you plunk things down louder than they need to be plunked.

When you pour tomato sauce out of the can, it's all flowing and it just trickles right into whatever you're cooking, like a little waterfall. But the tomato paste is thick and goopy, and you have to scrape it out with a spoon because you don't want to waste any and then your fingers get all sticky, and you never really get *all* of it out of the can because it's so hard to work with. Those were the two sides of Nina: sometimes all easy and smooth, and other times so stubborn and messy. I never knew which one I was going to get.

In the morning, after she came down the stairs and poured herself a bowl of cereal, Nina said, "Oh, Dad, I forgot to tell you. Mom asked about you."

Dad put the newspaper down.

"Yeah. At Thanksgiving. She said, 'Where is James? Why doesn't he ever come?'"

Dad's eyes cut over to me.

"No," I said. "She didn't say that."

Nina stood up and threw down her bowl, which smashed into pieces on the floor. Milk got all over the place.

"Steffany," she said, "you are *such* a butt-kisser."

She banged upstairs, and her bedroom door boomed shut. The light fixture over the kitchen table shook.

Fully Cooked

Nina rode way ahead of me that morning. It was tricky to steer my bike and wipe my cheeks at the same time. My sister was really the only one in the world who could ever understand my whole life, and when she was mad at me, I just didn't know what to do with myself.

The day dragged. In English, while taking notes on introductory paragraphs, body paragraphs, and concluding paragraphs, I got all in knots thinking about what Christmas would be like this year. Maybe Dad would invite Carol and those three guys, but it was hard to picture them around the same table as Auntie Gina and Harry.

Mrs. Ashton said that after winter break we needed to

turn in an outline of what we'd say in our autobiography letter, that we could just go into our notebooks that we've been writing in all year and take that stuff and make it into an outline. All that was in my notebook was a bunch of lists of grocery store stuff and recipe ideas. I had so much work to do and still didn't know exactly where I'd start.

After school I rode home by myself because Nina had dance, and for dinner that night I made chicken Parmesan with store-bought, premade, and already-breaded chicken breasts. They said "Fully Cooked" on the package. You just put sauce and then mozzarella and Parmesan cheeses all over them and put them in the microwave. To be a little fancy, I sprinkled Italian-ish herbs on top, like parsley, oregano, and basil.

I didn't want to overdo it though. After the Kitchen Sink meal fiasco, I was nervous about cooking and wondered if I was just bad at it after all and nobody ever told me. Making something easy and precooked that night made me feel better, like I couldn't mess it up. I boiled store-bought spaghetti to go with it, and Nina got dropped off just when I was taking the garlic bread out of the broiler.

"If you're gonna borrow my scarf, tell me first," she said, before she went up to her room. She didn't even give me a chance to say I didn't even know I put hers on and not mine.

Dad came in right after.

"Hey," he said.

"Hey," I said. He put his keys in the dish and then stood there in the doorway for just a second longer than normal.

"Mmmm," he said, taking a big whiff of the dinner. His cheeks were all red, and when he passed me on the way to the fridge, there was the smell. I never knew that smell until Dad: beer breath.

Nina came down, and I put the food on the table. For some reason, we all just sat there for a second before anyone started helping themselves. Then Dad said, "You guys been out to your Grandpa Falcon's old house? My old house? Man, it looks terrible. The whole yard is overgrown. The weeds spring up so high and tower into the air, about three feet, it looks like." He lifted up his hand to about where he thought three feet would hit.

"Grandpa built that path that used to go up to the front door—I remember when he did that. Now you can barely see it. Those people need a Weedwacker." He stabbed a piece of chicken with his fork and shook it off onto his plate.

"You guys," he said, shaking his head. "You guys are like these two people in my life that I have no idea how to be around. You guys are like these two . . . things I'm trying to win over, and I just don't know how. It's like I'm . . . I'm tossing the darts, and I never hit the bull's-eye."

"Um," said Nina, "what are you talking about?"

"I'm talking about me coming back here," he said as he stood up and went to the fridge. "I want this to work out.

I need this to work out. What can I do to make this work out?" he asked as he twisted the top off a bottle.

"Okay," said Nina. "You asked." She counted on her fingers. "Number one: stop being a loser. Number two: get a real job. Number three: don't drink all that beer. Number four: Mom . . ."

"Nina, that's not any way to talk to—"

"Don't tell me what way to talk to you. You were gone for—"

"Nina, shut up," said Dad.

"You shut up," she shouted. "I hate you, Dad. I really hate you." She ran upstairs.

Dad stood by the fridge, drinking his beer in these long, steady gulps.

Dad, I know what you mean about having no idea how to be around us.

He pulled another bottle out of the fridge and walked to the door.

We have no idea how to be around you, too.

The chicken Parmesan and I watched as he grabbed his keys, turned the knob, and disappeared. Why was it so hard for me to say anything? I wished I could have my words prerecorded or precooked like tonight's chicken. Then I'd just open them up, take them out, and serve them to whoever I needed to talk to—no big, messy kitchen full of measuring cups and sauce stains and flour spills.

I went up to Nina's room and knocked. She didn't answer. I knocked again, louder.

"What," she said. I could barely hear her.

"Can I come in?" I called.

"Fine," she said. I opened the door and peeked in. She was in the dark, sitting on her bed. I just stood in the doorway.

"What," she said.

"He left," I said. "He's not here."

She fell onto her back.

"I don't care," she said. "Good."

"But what are we gonna do?"

"I don't know," she said. "Just go to bed."

"Should we call Gina?"

"She doesn't care."

"Yeah, she does."

"Call her." She turned onto her side and reached up to click on her lamp. "Close the door, please."

"But . . ."

"Stef, just leave me alone," she said very quietly.

"But, can't I just—"

"Leave," she yelled. And this ballet shoe snow globe came flying at me but smashed against the wall and shattered. A dark, wet spot started to grow on the carpet where the pieces landed.

"Get out!" she shouted.

"Fine!" I said.

She got up off the bed and straddle-walked around the broken bits of glass and water and pushed the door closed almost on my face.

I walked straight down the hall toward Dad's room. I barged in and opened a dresser drawer. Pants. I opened another drawer. Shirts. He had actually unpacked stuff. Socks. A few pairs of shoes and even some shirts hanging in the closet. Near the crumpled bedspread that lay at the foot of the bed I sat down. I noticed the trumpet case standing in the corner.

Even though we talked to Auntie Gina often on the phone and went to dinners over there, she was so busy and far away in her new life. I wanted her here, now, and I wanted to tell her everything, but I just couldn't even imagine saying the words. Plus, I had been trying to *not* need her since September.

Something Big at Sausage-and-Pepper Night

In the days leading up to winter break, it was weird trying to act normal. It was a pushing-down feeling, the way you shoved down Jack in a jack-in-the-box. There were stiff springs fighting you as you pushed, but you just pushed harder.

Waking up each morning to Dad at the table with his coffee. Like nothing happened, like he didn't come home late the night of Kitchen Sink, like he didn't tell Nina to shut up and then leave the house. Riding bikes with Nina to school. Like nothing happened, like she didn't lie about what Mom said, like she didn't throw the cereal bowl and the snow globe.

There were lots of things to keep me busy, thank goodness. Some annoying, some fun. Annoying: that dumb outline for the autobiography was hanging over me. Fun: me and Lisa made caramel corn one day after school for the holiday party (we made a whole extra batch for Principal Schmitz-Brady). Lisa spent the night the weekend before the break. I had to get in as much Lisa time as I could, because she would be gone the whole break visiting her cousins in Portland. Also fun was the Faculty Kazoo Concert, and then on the first Saturday of break, after Dad went to work, me and Nina and Auntie Gina and Harry decorated the living room.

Last year's pine smell poured from the Christmas boxes. There were the blue bulbs and my construction paper stocking that said STEF in glitter. Tinsel and old candy canes. This big stuffed Santa that Mom knitted one year when I was really little—I don't remember Christmas without it. Just like I don't remember Mom anywhere but in the Place.

I was glad Dad wasn't there, because it was hard to imagine him hanging tinsel and singing along to Frank Sinatra's holiday hits, but I also didn't know how it'd ever truly feel right in me that *this* was my family if we could never be in the same places at the same times.

Auntie Gina was all giggling, and she was even wearing eye makeup. While Harry and Nina were wrapping the lights around the tree, me and Auntie Gina were in the kitchen getting dinner ready. I let myself forget that at the end of it she would go back home and we would be here with Dad, not knowing how he'd be when he walked in the door.

But for now, rolling up cooked sausages in pizza dough for sausage-and-pepper rolls made me feel like everything was okay. When there was flour on my forearms and olive oil on my fingers, and when the kitchen counter was all cluttered up with the cutting board and the pepper stems and the empty pizza-dough bags and the spices, there were words right in my mouth ready to say. I thought I would tell Auntie Gina about Dad. Nina hadn't said anything, because maybe she thought she might get in trouble. So I'd open my mouth, and I'd tell. Yeah. Not on Nina, just about Dad. It felt like it would be okay to do that.

But then right after we put the sausage rolls in the oven, Auntie Gina said she had something to tell us. Something big. She said to sit down. Before I even had the chance to get nervous, she blurted it out.

"Harry and I . . . are getting married!"

They were there, standing and holding hands by the tree and waiting for us to be happy, and there was the one *you left* part of me and the other *it's Christmastime* part of me, and both parts were trying to win, and I couldn't even make my lips or my face move.

"And we want both of you guys to be bridesmaids in the wedding, and Steffy, we would love it if you would bake our cake for us. If you would like to. If it wouldn't be too much. Would you? Like to?"

She got into her purse and pulled out two magazines with cakes on the covers and offered them to me. I took them and nodded. Nina was off the couch and hugging Harry and then jumping up and down with Auntie Gina and looking at the ring. A purple stone set in this old-fashioned flowery silver band. I hadn't even noticed it.

She said they were going to New York for Christmas this year because Harry's grandmother was still hanging on and there were some more relatives who would be there from Korea. Nina was saying stuff about the dress and how Auntie Gina would do her hair. I forced out congratulations.

She would be in New York for Christmas. She would be gone again. She kept leaving again and again and again in different ways. After they left that night and Dad was home and we were in our rooms, I shoved the cake magazines to the back of my closet.

Gnocchi with Nina

We usually had spaghetti on Christmas, but this year I was making gnocchi. And for the very first time it would be just me, Nina, and Dad for dinner. Auntie Gina was making new traditions, so we had to, too.

I got up early. On Christmas morning when we were little, we'd run into Auntie Gina's room and she'd walk out yawning in her robe and we'd scream when we saw the presents from Santa.

We'd exchanged gifts with Auntie Gina before she left. I loved my gift card to the Extra Ingredient, this fancy kitcheny store, and all my new clothes and shoes and the cookbooks and the cake pans. But I would rather have had her there for

Christmas and nothing under the tree than woken up that morning to those presents in a quiet house.

After turning the TV on to holiday cartoons (but keeping the volume on low so I didn't wake anybody), I got out the mashed potatoes that I'd made the night before and dumped them into a bowl. I scooped in flour and mixed. I sprinkled in some salt. I had never made this by myself before, but Auntie Gina was in New York without us, and what else was I going to do? It was *Christmas*. Nina didn't cook much, and I'd only ever seen Dad make coffee and toast. Plus, I'd watched and helped Auntie Gina make pasta a thousand times, so I guessed I'd just somehow figure it out.

I added the eggs and started kneading. The dough was all hard, though, and I remembered a tip Auntie Gina once said: if you're having trouble with dough, add a little water to help combine the ingredients. I did this, and it got a little easier. I thought of her thick fingers in the dough, her hands rhythmically folding, rolling, pressing, folding, rolling, pressing, like it was the easiest thing in the world to do. Her drinking coffee from one of the Christmas mugs, the three of us settling on the couch later in the morning for presents.

Kneading turned out to be really hard, and there came a point when I wanted to throw the dough in the trash and start over. When I felt like it was going all wrong, like I couldn't handle it because it was too thick and sticky to do anything with. I felt like that fat, blobby, scrappy dough was my life. Like I couldn't control it or make it right, how it was supposed to be.

Nina came down, yawning.

"Merry Christmas, Steffy," she said.

"Merry Christmas."

She was smiling and rubbing her eyes. "Mmmm," she said, looking at the dough. Her just saying that made me determined. There were all these nooks and craters in the dough, and it looked messy like the moon. While Nina made me a waffle, I just kept kneading. Finally, after what felt like four hours, I got it into a whole ball with not too many creases and crevices.

"Is it ready to cleesh?" asked Nina.

"I think so," I said. "Finally." I fell into a chair and wiped my forehead.

"You need a Pop-Tart," said Nina.

"I do," I said. My wrists were sore, and my fingers were throbbing. But I did it. I took those three separate ingredients (flour, eggs, and mashed potatoes) and joined them into this one big ball of dough.

After a frosted blueberry Pop-Tart, it was time to rub a little olive oil on the dough and then put it under a bowl for thirty minutes to cleesh. I don't know where the word really came from. Auntie Gina said it all the time about recipes, how the ingredients had to cleesh: to allow everything to fully marry up and come together.

We watched some of *A Christmas Story* for a little bit, one of our very, very favorite movies of all time. Then it was time to get back to the dough. We could really tell a difference after it cleeshed: it just felt like Play-Doh when it was all fresh and you took it out of the little canister for the first time.

I cut off a small slab, flattened it out with a rolling pin, and sliced it into long strips. Nina sat at the table with me while I did this, and after I sliced, she cut up the strips into little squares. Then we schweeted. That was another one of Auntie Gina's words. You just pressed into each piece with your finger and kind of pulled it toward you, like you were trying to wipe a little stain off the table with one swoop, only there's a gnocchi between your finger and the table. For each time we did it, we said, "Schweet." We just did. After a while, you could get into a rhythm and schweet pretty fast. Even though it took over an hour to do all the dough, we were doing it together. Me and Nina were laughing so hard at each other because when we would say "Schweet," we would try and say it in the weirdest, highest, or lowest voice each time, and one time Nina made me put down the knife because I was laughing so hard. It ended up being one of the best Christmas mornings.

"Nina," I said. I opened my mouth, and just air came out. "I have this dumb project for Mrs. Ashton."

"The autobiography?" she said, wiping flour into the trash can with a paper towel.

"Yes!"

"Yeah, we did that in fifth grade. I liked it. Gina wrote me my letter, I remember."

"She did?"

"Yeah, are you gonna ask her to write yours?"

"I don't know. I was gonna—ask you to."

"I'm not asking Gina for you."

"No, I was gonna ask you—to write it for me."

"I can't write your letter for you, as Gina."

"Nina," I said, laughing now. "I wanted you to write it for me, as *you*."

"Oooooh," she said. We looked right at each other. She put her arm around me for a second. "Yeah. Sure."

We scrubbed the rest of the flour off the table. That was done, finally. And so were the gnocchi. Right when we had gotten the kitchen back to normal, the doorbell rang, which scared me for some reason. Nina put her ear to the door and said, "Who is it?" and a voice said, "Your daddy's friend Carol." Nina looked at me. "From Thanksgiving," said the voice. I raised my eyebrows, and Nina opened the door and then the screen door and invited her in.

"Merry Christmas," she said. We said it back, and she handed us a paper plate covered with tinfoil. "Baked you guys muffins."

"Oh, thanks," I said, taking them and putting them on the counter.

"They're gonna be nothing compared to what you can do in the kitchen," she said to me.

"You haven't tasted everything I've done in the kitchen," I said. She smiled.

She said she'd walk us to church to meet Jean Sawyer for our ride to Mom's, because Dad was still asleep and nobody wanted to go wake him up. Carol said she had choir practice at the church this morning anyway.

Choir practice?

I loaded up my backpack with the gifts me and Nina had picked out for Mom and Helen, and headed out with her and Carol. I couldn't think of anything to say on the way—there was too much going through my head. Was Carol Dad's *girlfriend* or something?

I thought back to meeting her at Thanksgiving dinner. How she had brought over those loaves for making garlic bread, how I had liked that so much. How she didn't get mad when I spilled gravy on her pants. How she'd brought us muffins that morning. Truth was, I liked Carol. But if I liked Carol, would that make me against Mom?

While I was trying to make sense of all this, Nina was finding things to ask her about. Where she was from (Charlotte), and if she ever went to Greensboro Grasshoppers games like we did in the summer (yes). Carol asked us how school was and we said fine, and she asked us how Dad was and we said fine, and then no one said anything until we got to St. Theresa's.

It was pretty empty except for the lady in the office because it was between masses. After we said thank you to Carol, she headed down to the basement for choir practice. A couple other people were coming into the vestibule and then going down, too. It seemed strange that they had practice on Christmas.

Choir practice.

Was Dad in the choir?

Had Carol come over looking for Dad so they could go to choir practice together? I just couldn't imagine that. I couldn't imagine that at all. But maybe. He did play the trumpet—he *was* a music person, so maybe he could sing, too. But why wouldn't he tell us he was in the choir? Something felt fishy. I definitely couldn't imagine Carol in a choir. For one thing, her voice was all scratchy, and it sounded like sandpaper when she spoke, maybe from all the smoking. So I couldn't imagine her singing voice sounding that pretty.

There wasn't enough time to wonder about it right then. We got in the car with Jean and ate hunks of this coffee cake that she had baked. Still warm. And perfect.

"Jean, why can't we hire you to be our personal chef?" said Nina.

"Mmmm-hmmm," I said, through a mouthful of cake.

"I don't think I'm anywhere near the chef that Steffy is," she said, winking at me in the rearview mirror.

At the Place, hallway D was all decorated with tinsel and

cutout candy canes and stockings, and the rec room tree was blinking with tiny white lights.

"Hey there," said Helen, tipping her Santa hat to us. "Merry Christmas, ladies. Your two girls," she told our mom.

Mom stood up from the couch and hugged each of us hard. We gave her kisses and sat on either side of her on the couch. Right when we got comfortable, me and Nina looked at each other. There were the real bad days, and when the smell of Mom hit us, we knew this was one of them. She was all wet down in front.

"Mom," Nina said, "let me help you to the bathroom."

"I'm fine," she said. "Listen to this, girls," she said. "The letters are *L*, *U*, *E*, and *Y*. The clue is, 'smoldering on the holiday fire.'" A newspaper tear-off was on a magazine that sat in her lap. She chewed her eraser.

"Yule," said Nina.

"Yule!" Mom said, and she started erasing. We watched her erase and erase and erase what she had written, and the newspaper got thinner and thinner and thinner and started to get a hole in it. "Damn it," she said. "Damn it, damn it, damn it." Then Mom said a bad word that I'd never ever heard her say before. Me and Nina looked at each other.

"Mom," said Nina, standing up and holding out her hand. "Come on."

"No," she said. She wiped her eyes and threw the pencil.

Helen was right there in a second. "Come now," she said.

"Put it down for now. Put it down." She took the magazine and word scramble from my mom and picked up the pencil. "It's okay. Girls, this morning your mama played 'Let There Be Peace on Earth' from memory."

We said all the "good job" stuff we're supposed to say. Helen knelt in front of Mom.

"What's the matter, honey?" she asked.

"It's Christmas, and I want to go home," said Mom. Helen put her arms around her. "Come on," Helen said. "Let's get you cleaned up." She got Mom up, and they headed down the hallway. Nina got out her phone right away and called Denise, and I watched a little boy slap one of the residents about a hundred high fives.

Helen came and told us we could probably go ahead and be on our way soon. "Don't let today worry you," she said. "Holidays always put people in a funk around here." She straightened her hat, and the little white ball on the end bounced around. "But don't sweat it," she said. "She'll be all right."

Mom came back out in new clothes, and after a little more hanging out and doing word scrambles, we gave them their gifts. Helen opened her candle, and Mom opened her word search puzzle books. Being there with Mom today made me sad, and I felt mean, but I really wanted to get back to the gnocchi. I had a good feeling about those gnocchi, my very first on-my-own-cooked pasta meal.

When we got home later, Dad's bedroom door was open,

and his damp towel hung in the bathroom. But Dad wasn't there.

Jean had come in with us to see our tree and said, "Oh goodness, you've done it again, Steffany." I showed her all the gnocchi, and she put down the other coffee cake that she'd baked for us.

"I bet you can't stay," I said.

"Hon, it's the same old story at the Sawyers': cooking for a million people. Uncle Bennet's up from Raleigh, the Padgets are down from Charlottesville. You name 'em, we've got 'em. If you hadn't gone to town in your own kitchen, you and your dad and Nina'd be coming over, too. But listen, y'all are gonna have a great Christmas this year. I know it," she said. And after a big squeeze, she was gone.

I turned on the tree lights and Frank Sinatra's holiday hits. I was stirring the sauce when Nina came into the kitchen.

"Okay," she said, "Denise's mom just invited us for Christmas."

"That's so nice," I said. "Maybe on another holiday we could go."

"Well, I was kind of thinking we should go," said Nina.

"What?"

"Stef . . . let's just go. It'll be fun. Denise actually has a trampoline in her backyard."

"So?" I said. "Dad's coming back soon, and we're having gnocchi. That we made."

"Stef," she said. She looked around the kitchen and lifted

her hands in the air. "I don't know where Dad is. Do you?"

"No."

"If we go to Denise's, we won't be by ourselves on Christmas."

"We're not by ourselves. We're with each other."

"Steffany, you don't get it. Dad doesn't want to be here. He never did." She started texting. Then her phone rang. Before I could say anything, she was on the phone telling Denise we'd actually love to take her up on that, and thank you.

"Wait," I said. "Nina." She was still talking and waved me away. "Nina!"

She got up off the bar stool and walked into the living room. I followed her.

"I'm not going," I mouthed to her. She held up one finger while she finished talking. Then she hung up.

"Steffy," she said, tilting her head to the side. "Just come."

"I don't want to. I want to stay. And . . . and you can't leave on Christmas."

"Stef," she said, "you have your chance to come and have a really nice dinner."

"I'm *making* a really nice dinner," I said. "You helped."

She sighed. "I know," she said. She glanced at all the gnocchi on the counter, waiting to be boiled up. "We'll bring the gnocchi."

"What?"

"Yeah."

"You can't just *bring* gnocchi somewhere. You have to

cook it. We have to cook it. Here. In our house."

"Stef," said Nina. "Turn off the sauce. Go pack a sleepover bag. And come with me. Come on."

While she headed upstairs, I just stood there. The sauce simmered on the stove. There was a loaf of Italian bread waiting to be smeared with butter and chopped garlic. I thought we could play cards or something, or watch a movie and eat caramel corn after dinner. It was the first time that we had made a whole pasta meal without Auntie Gina. And we had really done it.

Nina came back down carrying her backpack and went straight to the front door.

"You coming?" she asked. I shook my head. Her eyes were watery, and she was wiping her nose with a tissue. She had put on lots of eyeliner.

She looked up at the star on the tree and said, "I'm sorry, Steffy." Her bottom lip was shaking. "This is the meanest thing I've ever done, and I know it. And I don't know why I have to go so much. Except I just can't be here, in our house, without Auntie Gina. Sorry."

She was out the door. I heard her bike being wheeled from the garage out to the street. Her *bike*? We weren't even supposed to go to Mom's on our bikes. And where did Denise live? I sat down and held my stomach. Well, fine. She could go to dumb Denise's for some dumb dinner. Probably it would be bad. It'd be me and Dad, just as soon as he got home.

Later, after the gnocchi were boiled, the garlic bread

warmed, and the salad tossed, I sat. And sat. I watched *It's a Wonderful Life*, which is a very, very, very long movie. The sun had disappeared. The news came on.

"Dad," I said.

The word just sat there in the air.

"Dad?"

I yelled for him. I was on the couch, holding a pillow on my stomach, squeezing it, calling for Dad. Where could he have gone on Christmas? And why did Nina leave? Why did Harry have to ask Auntie Gina to marry him?

The dinner had been waiting on the table for hours and I just left it there. I didn't feel like gnocchi. I felt like an artichoke, is what I felt like. I felt like an artichoke that all the leaves had been pulled off of, and I was just a heart. Whenever we'd made artichokes together, Auntie Gina would say she liked the heart best.

I walked to the front door holding the pillow tight and locked the dead bolt. I wondered what New York was like at Christmastime and what Auntie Gina was doing right then, if she was having dinner at a big table with all of Harry's relatives.

I called Nina's cell and could barely leave a message, my voice was all quivery. "Dad's still not home," I just said. "Everything got cold."

For the rest of Christmas, I hid in Nina's bed with Wiley, half awake, my stomach growling. Every light in the house on. TV downstairs full blast.

Coffee and Sauce

I heard snoring when I woke up. I had left Nina's door open, but I didn't hear him come in. The TV was off, and the sun was just starting to peek through Nina's blinds. I squeezed Wiley to me and closed my eyes again. I didn't want to think about anything.

Then I woke up to both the smells of coffee and sauce. Light was flooding into Nina's room. I pulled myself out of her bed and headed downstairs with Wiley. On the table were Dad's mug with steam rising from it and a bowl of warmed gnocchi.

He looked at his hands when he said, "Hey."

I said, "Hey."

I was by myself on Christmas, I missed you, I made dinner, where were you?

He picked a scab on his knuckle and said, "Where's Nina?"

And I said, "Denise's." The knuckle bled. There was a bloody tissue wrapped around his other knuckles. And on the side of his face was a long cut, like someone took a slice out of his skin. There was also his eye. It had a black-and-blue ring underneath it.

The Greensboro that I lived in was a different place from the world of Dad. And I didn't know if it'd ever feel like he was going to be able to be in my Greensboro. There was this feeling like a door closing inside of me, this tightening up, and I realized how hard I was squeezing Wiley. I kind of felt, right then—more than I had even felt when Dad first came back—that I knew Mr. Richmond, my math teacher, better than I would ever know him.

We sat across from each other, him slurping his coffee, me staring at the big bowl of gnocchi in front of him. Two flavors that should never be served together in the same meal.

More Ginger Ale, Anyone?

All during the rest of break, it kind of felt like they wanted to say sorry, but they just didn't. For Christmas, Nina did give me a cookbook and these orange spatula earrings. And Dad was up early, every day of the week after Christmas, getting ready for work.

Even though I missed the mornings when he'd read the paper and I'd make eggs, I stayed in bed. I didn't want to sit and try and think of something to say. I didn't want to see the scabs on his knuckles or the way that his black eye bruise was turning yellow. Plus there were the leftover gnocchi to face.

On the night before we went back to school, I made macaroni and cheese and soup. Dinner went like this:

"So," said Nina, "I'm sleeping over at Denise's after dance tomorrow and Tuesday, and then I'll just go to school with her in the mornings."

"I can pick you up from the studio," said Dad.

"You don't have a car."

"We can take the bus," he said.

"No. I'm doing it this way," said Nina.

"I'm having more ginger ale," I said.

"Nina, I can pick you up. It's too many nights out. School nights."

"No, it's not," said Nina.

"More ginger ale?"

"Nina, no," said Dad.

"You wanna talk about too many nights out, James? You can't tell me what to do." Nina was grasping her fork, tight.

"I'm in charge here," said Dad.

"Not of me." She said this with a too-sweet voice, and got up and put her dish in the sink. Then she went to her room. Dad stood up and threw down his napkin.

"Nina," he called as he headed upstairs. I heard him knock on her bedroom door. And wait. And knock. And knock again. And wait. Then the hallway floor creaked as Dad went to his room. His door clicked shut.

As the warm water ran over the pots, I went through all the things I should say and ask. For some reason, I could yell and yell for Dad when I knew he wasn't here, but I couldn't say anything to either of them for real. Nobody around here was saying anything that they should. It was just this feeling of everyone being kind of mad, but instead of blowing up, they were just letting it simmer.

After I washed the pots and put everything else in the dishwasher, I knew I should go and do homework that I put off all break—there were these math worksheets and the autobiography outline—but instead I went online and read about rotini pasta in ricotta and mozzarella cheeses. It was the only thing I wanted to do.

While I was clicking around, this thing popped up that said: "Chefs of Tomorrow, Greensboro, NC." I clicked on the cartoon of a kid wearing big, green oven mitts. It was a cooking contest for kids, right here in Greensboro. I sort of read the information but then the trumpet started. That same song from before that Nina had danced to. Then there was this pounding that made me jump. Nina yelled something from her room about homework. It got quiet again. Too bad. I would've liked to hear that song again.

The autobiography outline was nagging at me, so I left the Chefs of Tomorrow website, and I opened my notebook. Still, all my notes were just ingredients and recipes. It sort of hit me that your life was basically a giant recipe—that you decided all the ingredients that you wanted to put into it, like for me cooking and riding my bike and hanging out with Lisa and my family, and for Nina dance and Denise, and for Dad playing the trumpet and I guessed painting houses. And maybe us. Kind of.

It made me wonder what Mom's ingredients had been. It made me wonder if she ever felt sad that she never got to make a real meal out of her life. And I closed my notebook and went to bed. I hoped Mrs. Ashton would accept a list of ingredients instead of an outline for now, because that was all I had.

Farm-to-Table

The first day at school after New Year's, it felt like some of me was still at home, fighting coming back. Some of me was back in my room, wondering about my mom and her life, worrying about Dad and Nina and everything that was festering between them. But the other part of me was there at school, trying to pretend everything was normal, that we'd had a good break.

Right before community meeting, Lisa handed me a little square of newspaper that her mom had cut out. It said "Chefs of Tomorrow," with the cartoon of the oven mitt kid.

"My mom made me bring it," she said. "It's your destiny." I couldn't help laughing at that. "Look," she said, pointing to the cutout, "you have to make a main course and a dessert using a common ingredient."

I read out loud: "'A parent or guardian must sign off in good faith that the child was the true chef.'" Right then I was back in my room hugging Wiley, wishing Auntie Gina, my guardian for eight official years, had never left. I didn't know if Lisa could read my mind or something, because right away she said: "Oh, don't worry about that. Your dad'll do it. Or your aunt. And look here," she said, running her finger under a few lines. "If you get picked for the finals, you have to go back and make your thing again on TV!"

"What?" I said, reading on. "Oh my gosh. And the winner gets their meal put on the menu at Lucky Thirty-Two?" I read on. "'Greensboro's finest farm-to-table dining establishment'?"

"And three thousand dollars," said Lisa. My jaw dropped.

All that money? And Lucky 32? I'd never been there, but "farm-to-table" reminded me of the rich flavor of the eggs from Grandpa Falcon's chickens compared to the kind of flat taste of Harris Teeter eggs. Farm-to-table was straight cooking from actual things you grew in your very own yard, and that was Grandpa Falcon all the way. The memory of making mud pies in Grandpa's backyard while he pulled up potatoes made this whole contest seem like it was something I had to do no matter what.

After community meeting, Principal Schmitz-Brady

came and pulled me aside. I got all jittery when her hand went on my shoulder.

"Ms. Sandolini," she said. "Chefs of Tomorrow. Look it up."

I showed her the clipping from Lisa's mom.

"Are you interested?" she asked. I nodded.

"That's a girl," she said, heading off toward the gym's exit. Lisa convinced me to go with her to the library at lunch, and we pulled up the contest's website.

"Here," she said, clicking on age group nine to twelve. I filled everything out. When I got to the bottom of the screen, it said I had to have a grown-up present to sign up.

"I can't do this now, I guess," I said.

"Oh yeah, you can. You just say you're your parent or guardian." It was true. Basically you just had to click Yes—that you were the parent or guardian and that you gave permission—and then you got taken to the next screen.

Lisa grabbed my hand and made my finger click Submit.

"Oh my gosh," I said."I can't believe I just did that."

"Believe it," said Lisa.

I printed out a copy of the application receipt and got an idea. Since I'd planned on showing Mrs. Ashton my ingredients list instead of an official outline, I thought I could also show her my Chefs of Tomorrow application.

In English class, after we'd handed in our outlines and during journaling, I went up to her desk.

"Yes, Stef?"

"Um, I turned in something . . . that's not quite an outline."

"Okay," she said.

"It's . . . it's a thing that is about me but hasn't happened yet, but I know I'll write about it. For the autobiography. Is that okay?"

"I'll look at it tonight, and if it's a problem, I'll let you know. Sound good?"

"Yes."

"Thanks for letting me know," she said.

Okay. At least I had turned in something. Thank goodness for the Chefs of Tomorrow thing. Thank goodness for Lisa and her mom and Principal Schmitz-Brady.

That night I told Dad and Nina all about what I did and showed them the application. When I was finished, there was quiet for a second, and then Nina was talking and then Dad was talking.

"Oh my God, Steffany, that's perfect for you," said Nina.

"You're kidding me!" said Dad. "That contest was made for you."

"I'm voting gnocchi," said Nina.

"If you want to show them something really Southern, you have to do Brussels sprouts and egg whites," said Dad.

"Eeew," said Nina. "No, Italian food. It's more complicated and impressive that she can make that. For eggs, all you do is fry them, right, Steffy?"

"Well, kind of," I said, "but you have to season them, too."

I could have talked about recipes with them all night long. Nina didn't have a mean tone, and Dad was grinning. All my insides felt lighter—maybe I could go to school tomorrow without feeling all weighted down with worry.

I couldn't sleep because I was imagining all sorts of meals I could try to cook. It dawned on me while looking at my clock (9:57 p.m.) that I needed to go through my mom's *Better Homes and Gardens* cookbook. I mean, *really* go through it to find her best recipes in there. There was a fat pile of handwritten ones shoved under the front cover. It was the first week of January. The contest was Saturday, March 30. I had three months to figure it out.

I turned my pillow over and got comfortable on my stomach, and my mind wandered over to the little detail that I'd skipped when I was telling Dad and Nina about Chefs of Tomorrow—how I said on the online sign-up that I was my own parent or guardian. How I never wanted that to feel true again.

The Great Cupcake Burst

What was weird about all those tons of handwritten or newspaper-clipping recipes under the front cover of my mom's cookbook was that there were no pasta recipes written out at all in there. Or sauce. I guess if you were Italian you just had to watch your aunt a million times and then get your hands in the dough to learn, like I did.

The more I made those recipes, the less mad at my dad and Nina I was. Working hard at cooking and baking was making the grudge break up into pieces and fall away. I just started to get really into Chefs of Tomorrow. My entry had to be the best thing I could make, so I was practicing a lot. I hadn't yet figured out what my "common ingredient" would be, but I knew it would come to me. It had to.

Me and Dad and Nina spent every night that winter eating a new dish I had prepared from Mom's cookbook. One night Nina got invited to Denise's, but she ended up inviting Denise over to our house instead so they could eat the turkey burgers I'd made. And Dad was coming home a little earlier than usual to see what was for dinner each night. Auntie Gina and Harry even started stopping over to test out a bite of my chicken and waffles (thumbs-up: fried chicken was perfect crispiness) or my barbecued pork chops (thumbs-down: pork chops were too tough). It was almost like a restaurant! Without waiters.

I was determined to figure out my common ingredient before March first. So one Friday in February when we had a half day for teacher meetings, Lisa slept over. We said we'd definitely have the ingredient all set by the time she left on Saturday.

After school, we got out my mom's cookbook, and Lisa closed her eyes and pulled out a wrinkly index card. In my mom's handwriting, it said, "Polenta—Italian cornmeal porridge."

"Oooh yes!" I said. "We have a big bag of this in our pantry."

"Let's do it," said Lisa.

Just like the recipe said, we boiled water, added a dash of salt, and then poured in the polenta.

Lisa read from the card: "'Keep stirring for a few minutes until it thickens.'"

We took turns stirring the whole time it was on the heat. After a little while, it started to look and feel like cookie dough.

"Oh crap," I said. "It's too thick."

"Uh-oh," said Lisa as she peeked into the big pot. "Should we start again?"

"It's so much food to waste."

"How much water did we put in?" she asked.

"Four cups. Like it says."

"Let's do five this time," she said.

I turned off the heat and slumped onto a chair. "I don't even know my ingredient," I said.

"We're gonna figure it out. We are," she said. "Get off the chair and let's make it again. I've never had polenta. And I want to try it."

Lisa made us try again, this time using more water. When we stirred the pot, the consistency was more like porridge, like how it was supposed to be.

"See?" she said. "If at first you don't succeed—"

"Add water," I said.

With meat sauce on top, the polenta was just the right mix of the two flavors: salty sausage and sweet corn.

Since Dad wasn't home yet and Nina was having a peanut butter sandwich in front of the TV, it was just me and Lisa at the table.

"What about something with chocolate?" she asked. "Can you do a chocolate dessert, and . . . chocolate pasta?"

"Hmmm," I said. "Too weird."

"But, I mean," said Lisa, "what kind of dessert thing could you also put in a main course thing?"

"Well, let's think about vegetables," I said. "Sometimes there're vegetables that you could kind of put in a dessert. Like zucchini bread."

"Huh," Lisa said. "How about carrot . . . cake. And carrot . . . casserole!"

"I like it!" I said. "But . . . okay. I've never really done a casserole."

"Hmmm," said Lisa.

We sat there thinking for a second. Lisa closed her eyes and pulled out a folded piece of paper from my mom's cookbook.

She squinted at the page and read, "'Jeannie . . . Berry . . .'?" She stopped and looked closer. "Oh. 'Jeannie *Beannie's* Lemon Bars.' I love lemon bars."

"But what would be the main course?" I asked.

"Lemon chicken! It's on every Chinese restaurant menu!"

"That actually sounds good. Lemon chicken has so many flavors in it. I mean, think about it You have the sweet sauce plus the tartness of the acidy lemon plus the saltiness of the chicken. I like mixing flavors together that you wouldn't normally think would be good together."

"Let's think of more," said Lisa.

"Okay," I said. "Let's think of more that would involve pasta. I imagined myself making something pasta-ish."

"Yeah," she said. We thought for a second.

"Tomato pie for dessert and then . . . pasta with tomato sauce?" she said.

"Huh," I said. "Tomato pie . . . I don't know if that's a thing."

"Yeah," she said. "You know what we should do? We should start a dessert business."

"We should so start a dessert business," I said.

"Astronaut desserts," said Lisa.

"Yes! Even astronauts need dessert in space!"

"They eat these little packets of food that's all freeze-dried," she said. "My uncle who worked for NASA got us ice-cream-flavored ones once. They're the texture of Smarties, but even more chalky. They still taste like ice cream though."

"Hey," I said. "I have an idea. We're making cupcake balls."

"Yes!" said Lisa. "What's a cupcake ball?"

"I don't know yet," I said. "I just thought of it right now."

We started with a Betty Crocker chocolate cake mix. We did twenty-four cupcakes. Once they cooled off, we decided we'd eat a little hole at the bottom of each one and then fill it with frosting. Then we thought we'd ball them up, frosting in the center, and put them in the freezer overnight. Then we could package them up in Baggies and sell them.

But what happened was, when we started to ball up the first one, the frosting splurted right out and we both screamed. Lisa went to try and catch it, and it got all over her arm. And then she took the arm and she wiped chocolate frosting on my cheek. I gasped, and we stood there with our mouths open.

"Oooh," I said, "you are *so* in trouble." And I was smearing it in her hair, and she put more on my cheeks, and we were screaming and lunging at each other with handfuls of cupcake and frosting. The chocolate on my forehead and ears made me laugh nonstop. . . . There was a big blob on Lisa's nose.

Nina came into the kitchen and said, "Oh. My. God."

Dad got home from work when we were wiping chocolate off the fridge and the microwave. He stood there by the key dish for a second.

I squeezed my wet dishrag hard, remembering the one evening that he came home late, the evening he told Nina to shut up. But this night he walked right in, normal, even laughing at our chocolate war.

"Nice to see you, Lisa," said Dad. "That is you, underneath the chocolate?"

Lisa and I giggled. "Yeah," she said, wiping her chin with a paper towel.

"How's your dad?" he asked. "Still riding that motorcycle?"

"No," she said, "my mom just made him sell it."

"Aw, well. It's about time," Dad said. "He's had that thing since high school. Tell him I said hi. Speaking of cars," he said, pulling out his phone and flipping it open, "what do you guys think of this?"

It was a small red car. *$5200* was written in white on the driver's-side window. Nina leaned in and squinted at the small screen.

"Dad," she said, "you so need to upgrade your cell. Whose car is that?"

"Maybe ours," said Dad. "A friend of a friend is selling."

"Really?" Nina said.

Right then Denise got there, and all us girls headed upstairs. Nina closed her door behind her and Denise. In my room, me and Lisa made up a business plan for ourselves where we would cook space foods. We thought we could do a Space Chefs of Tomorrow kind of thing where the contestants had to think of one giant meal that astronauts could eat on the way to space, then once they got into space, then on the way back from space. Then we got bored with that and started acting out a cooking show we made up called *Baking for Bucks*.

I would never have been able to play something like that with Nina, and we had the best time ever. Lisa was making all these funny voices for each contestant on the cooking show. It was that kind of laughing where you are crying and you can't stop and it just fills up your whole stomach and throat and it feels like your face is going to burst. Because the more Lisa giggled, the more I giggled, but then the more I did, the more she did. Once Nina and Denise knocked on the door and told us to shush.

Getting My Hands in a Recipe

On Saturday morning, while me and Lisa were at the table eating waffles, that lady Carol came over, and she and Dad went outside together. They didn't go anywhere—they just were outside at the card table.

"What are they doing out there?" whispered Lisa.

"I'm not sure," I whispered back. We put down our forks, crept close to the window, and kind of crouched down. They were laughing at something. Then it got really quiet, but you could hear their voices a little bit.

I craned my neck forward and heard my dad say, ". . . I think . . . only person who wasn't waiting for me to fail . . ."

Me and Lisa looked at each other. We didn't hear any

more talking for a minute, so we went back to our waffles.

"We need my lunar-talkies," she said.

"Oh my gosh, yes," I said. Lisa was joking but I wasn't. If I could hear what they were saying, maybe I could find out what was going on with them.

"Carol is nice," Lisa said once we were sitting down again. She sprinkled a handful of blueberries on her second waffle.

"Yeah," I said, "but I don't get it."

"I know. It's like, what is it?" she asked. "Are they having a romance or something?" she whispered.

"I have no idea," I said. I didn't say that I was scared that maybe my dad and Carol were actually more than just friends. I didn't say the words that were buried somewhere in my gut—that maybe my dad didn't love my mom anymore. I felt stupid that I had never really thought about it before. But now that he was back at home and there was this lady around, it made me wonder. I didn't say the thing about them being in the St. Theresa's choir together. It was just too bizarre. First of all, was there a St. Theresa's choir? I'd never heard them sing at church.

We finished breakfast, and Lisa helped me put all the dishes in the sink and we soaked them. Then we noticed there were chocolate smears on the fridge still and wiped them off.

We went back and forth about the common ingredient

and finally agreed that it would have to be a vegetable.

"We'll figure it out, don't worry. You have plenty of time," she said. I knew she was right, and anyway, my mind was on other stuff.

A little while later, when Lisa's mom honked, I walked her to her car to say bye. Dad and Carol were still outside, sitting at the card table. Dad stood and waved to Lisa's mom, who waved back from their car. After they drove away, Dad said that he and Carol were probably going out for a little bit and they'd be back soon, and to lock the door when I went inside.

I did, but after turning the deadbolt, I didn't just go about my business normally. I crouched down again by the window, where I had listened with Lisa earlier. I put my head up as close to the window as possible without being seen and squinted so hard to somehow get their words into better focus in my ears.

Laughing. Then quiet. The flicky sound of Carol's cigarette lighter.

"No," said Dad. "I don't know how to deal with it yet," he was saying, but then he was too quiet to hear. I didn't believe I was doing this, but I climbed up on the counter so I could be closer to the window. My face was so close to the faucet that I had to be careful not to accidentally turn it on with my chin.

"Coming back to Greensboro, there are eyes all over

me," he said, "so many eyes. Too many eyes, waiting for me to mess up again."

It sounded like he was a voice on the phone or something, and the connection was kind of bad. Then he said something I couldn't hear.

There was quiet for a few seconds and then Carol said how one of her kids called her last night. And then she was talking for a minute and then they got up from the table, and their voices got fainter and fainter. Their shoes crunching the leaves on the grass told me they were walking away. Thank goodness, because I was getting a cramp in my neck.

I hopped down from the counter. I had to hear more. Ever since he told me they were going out for a while, I was kind of making a plan. Nina and Denise had gone to an early dance class, so I didn't have to tell her about it. Dad was gone, so he couldn't say no. I just didn't want to be alone in the house, so I made my own plan. And that was that.

I raced to St. Theresa's on my bike with all sorts of questions floating around inside. All the eyes on Dad of people waiting for him to mess up—did he think my eyes and Nina's eyes were part of those eyes? And that time when Dad was telling us about that one night, about the loud waves on the beach when he was alone—did he still feel alone like that, after coming back to Greensboro?

I also thought about how when Auntie Gina lived with us, we would have never gotten to just go off on our own.

Maybe we were old enough now. Maybe not. But it sure felt good. Something about being out, just as me, with no one telling me what to do, swelled me up with pride. I felt like this when I had my hands in some recipe, and I was shaping it and kneading it or breaking up meat. That feeling when you are throwing yourself into something, even if you don't know exactly how it's going to turn out in the end.

When I got to St. Theresa's, I couldn't lock up my bike fast enough. I slipped into the church as quiet as I could. It was calm in there—only a couple people and old ladies were in the pews here and there, sitting or kneeling, fingering rosary beads.

Then I did it. I tiptoed downstairs to the basement.

There was a coffee smell, and cigarette smoke. A long table with silver pots and milk cartons and Styrofoam cups and plates. Boxes of doughnuts and stacks of napkins. People sitting in rows toward the far end of the room. Dad and Carol were in the last row, talking quietly. I felt all smart that I guessed where they were that morning. I wished I could hear what they were saying.

But . . . choir practice? I imagined at a choir practice there would maybe be music stands or a piano, or someone with a guitar or something. There was none of that. And did they all know the songs by heart? A guy with a ponytail at the front of the group said, "We'll start in about fifteen minutes."

What were they going to start in about fifteen minutes?

People stretched their arms above their heads, and some stood from their chairs. Dad was one of them, and he started to turn around. Toward the stairwell. The smoke got in my throat, and there was a cough wanting to come out. I rushed up the stairs and out the door. I didn't think he saw me. I jumped on my bike and pedaled toward home so hard I had to adjust my gears.

The wind whipped past my cheeks as I flew down the sidewalk. There were a million questions flashing through my head. First, there was the basement stuff: what were they doing down there, exactly? And why wouldn't Dad just say where he was going? And then there was the Dad and Carol stuff: did they like each other like *that*? And what about Mom? I couldn't understand it. If you once loved someone, how could you just turn love off, like a faucet?

When She Wrote the Recipes Down

The smell of cold polenta hit me as I swung the fridge door open. It was late—my clock said 11:49 p.m. when I had gotten out of bed. I wasn't that hungry for a middle-of-the-night snack, but string cheese seemed kind of good. I ate it like a candy bar, not bothering to pull down little sections.

One car passed down a street nearby. The dogs next door barked. The refrigerator hummed. I crumpled up the cheese wrapper and threw it away. Then I got out my mom's cookbook and pulled out a photocopied sheet of paper from under the front cover.

"Yam-Pecan Pie," it said. "One cup mashed-up yams, one-third cup brown sugar, one-quarter teaspoon cinnamon."

I wondered if my mom was ever a get-up-in-the-middle-of-the-night person. I read all the pie ingredients and wondered how she came to have this recipe, if she'd asked for someone to copy it for her. I wondered if she'd ever made it for my dad.

I wondered if my dad had made any of these recipes for her. I never used to wonder so many things about him. Somehow, when he lived in California, I felt like it was easier to understand who he was: my dad, he lives in California, that's it.

But now that he was back in Greensboro and I saw him every day, he was harder to get: my dad, he goes out and doesn't say where he's going or when he'll be back. And because I was finding out I didn't understand him after all, I was determined to know him better.

I took out another recipe of my mom's. She watched me from her senior picture as I sat with the cookbook in my lap.

"Pizza Frittas—Italian Doughnuts." I remembered those. Auntie Gina had made them before. You fried up little pieces of pizza dough and then popped them in a bag with sugar in it and shook the bag around.

Then I took out the card that said "Polenta—Italian Cornmeal Porridge." I slid my finger along the words that she had written so many years ago and followed the writing all the way through the whole recipe.

"I'm like you," I said out loud to my mom's picture. My

voice was hoarse because it was late and I hadn't talked in hours. "I'm like you, but you don't know it."

I was wanting something so bad, something I knew I couldn't have. I was wanting my mom to just come out of that picture on the wall, just be how she was, come back to me and be my mom.

Wait a minute.

Mom. Polenta.

Being as quiet as I could, I got down a Tupperware from the cabinet over the sink. Then from the fridge, I took out the leftover polenta from last night. I spooned a good portion into the Tupperware, sealed up the container, and put it back in the fridge. There was this current running through me that I had started to feel yesterday when I rode to the church.

If all I had of Mom was her cookbook, maybe that was all she had of herself, too. Maybe if I started bringing her all those old recipes she used to cook, she'd start remembering when she made them, who was there, how the food tasted. *Who she was when she wrote them down. Who she is now.*

I imagined the scene at the Place tomorrow. I'd bring the polenta. Mom would eat some. She'd remember something about cooking it from when she was little. She would remember something about us. She would see us and know us. She would.

Potatoes and Yams and Bears, Oh My

When I woke up that Sunday morning, I sat up and said, "Potatoes," out loud.

"Potatoes are vegetables," I told Wiley. "There are different kinds of potatoes. There are yams, which are like sweet potatoes, and then there are normal potatoes, which are savory potatoes."

I squeezed Wiley. "But they're all potatoes!"

What is a main course that uses potatoes? Gnocchi!

What is a dessert that uses yams? Yam-pecan pie!

My entry for Chefs of Tomorrow = Gnocchi and Yam-Pecan Pie!

Downstairs, I took the pie recipe out of the cookbook

and read the ingredients again. I started a grocery list with yams at the top. I pulled open the baking cabinet to make sure that we had a new thing of brown sugar. In the fridge, I checked that the baking soda wasn't expired. As soon as I had all the ingredients, I'd do a test pie.

I had to call Lisa.

"Lisa," I said. "It's me. Thanks for getting me thinking about vegetables."

"What?"

"Yam-pecan pie and potato gnocchi!"

There was a pause.

"Stef," she said, "yes!"

We talked for a little more and then I had to go get dressed to go to the Place.

Before we left, no one asked me why I was putting a Tupperware from the fridge in my backpack. Good. It would be kind of hard to explain why I wanted my mom to have some of her old polenta-and-sauce recipe. But it made sense to me.

I felt sneaky, having Dad walk us over to the church since I had just ridden there by myself yesterday, but of course I didn't say anything about that. On the way, Dad and Nina talked about new-car stuff ("Does it have a sunroof?"). Ever since Chefs of Tomorrow and ever since Dad said he was getting a car, they were being friendly to each other, and somehow the grudge I had toward them had melted down to nothing.

When we got to Mom's, I went right up to Helen. "We brought a snack," I said. "I'm practicing for a cooking contest, so there are all these leftovers and . . . and it's her old recipe. Could you warm it up a little? Please?" I was losing my breath and had to take a gulp of air.

"Sure, dearie," said Helen. "What have we here?"

"It's polenta," I said. "Cornmeal porridge and pasta sauce." She nodded as she took the Tupperware and headed off down the hall. It wasn't just polenta. It was magic polenta. Stuff that Mom used to make for us before her injury. Maybe eating it and talking about it would bring back the memories that had been locked in her brain since she got hurt.

Mom sat on the couch with the newspaper in her lap, opened to the "Living" section. She glanced up at me and smiled a stranger smile.

"It's us, Mom," said Nina. "Your girls."

She closed the paper and reached out her hands.

"Hi, Steffy and Nina," she said. We hugged her and gave her kisses. Nina told her we were getting a new car, and I reminded her about Chefs of Tomorrow. I had told her weeks back, too, but had mentioned it every week since.

"I decided I'm doing potato gnocchi and yam-pecan pie," I said.

"Nice," said Nina.

"Good plan," Mom said. "I really, really want to be there. But I don't know. I think . . . I'm going to ask Helen if there's some way . . ." The corners of her mouth started to get pulled down. "Don't laugh," she said, "but it makes me nervous. Going outside."

"Mom," said Nina, "we would never laugh." Mom nodded and took Nina's hand. "We would be there, too, and we would help you."

Mom might come. Mom might come! And my dad would be there, too. Me, Nina, Mom, and Dad. Together. I stood up and walked over to the window for a minute, kind of holding my breath that that could actually happen. Mom and Dad together.

Then Helen came out with the warmed polenta on a plate.

"I knew I smelled something," Mom said. I got all jumpy as we walked her to the dining table.

"You used to make this all the time, Mom," I said. "Your sister, Gina, says you made it the best, next to your dad."

Mom took one bite and closed her eyes and chewed. Me and Nina sat there with her while she ate, and no one said a word. Nina glanced at me a couple times, and it was the old, real Nina, nothing in her eyes but hoping.

"Remember, Mom, I don't like it," said Nina. Mom leaned down close to the plate and breathed in big.

"Sauce," she said. "Mmmm."

"Yeah," said Nina. "Steffy made that. Auntie Gina says she makes it as good as you did. Do."

Mom looked sideways at Nina.

"But I don't like polenta," Nina said. "When I was little, you would make me macaroni and cheese when you'd make it." Nina bit her fingernails.

Mom scooped up the last bite and dabbed her mouth with the napkin. I imagined those chunks of cornmeal and sauce floating around inside of her, each one carrying a little memory trigger. I thought about my mom's brain and how her injury had sealed up pieces of her past in tight wrappers, how maybe there was some way to open them back up and take them out.

She leaned over to Nina and took her face in her hands and then kissed her. Then she reached out for my hand and gave me a squeeze. She squinted at us both real hard.

"Do you remember, Mom? Do you remember making polenta?" Nina asked.

"You know what I remember, honey?" Mom said. "I remember making sauce. I really do. Breaking apart the meat. And I remember that I didn't like polenta either when I was young. Just like you."

Nina was nodding and looking up and dabbing the bottoms of her eyes, smudging eyeliner on her fingers. Mom was like me in some ways. I knew it. And she was like Nina, too. It hit me right then how my sister remembered Mom better than me. How she was probably way sadder than me to come here and see her now.

We all three sat there together at the dining-room table, me and Nina holding Mom's hands while she studied our faces. I wondered if somehow, when she started to have more memories of us, we'd start to have more of her, too. If it was shared memories that held people together.

Dozens of Dinners and Desserts

March 30. It was here. Over the past three months, I had made dozens of dinners and desserts, and since I'd figured out my contest entry, I'd made seven batches of gnocchi and eight yam-pecan pies.

That morning I had been on the phone with Lisa three times and had changed outfits four times, and Nina had knocked on my door twice to hand me different shirts to borrow and put makeup on me. Gina and Harry were downstairs with Dad, putting tinfoil on all my stuff.

Nina knocked on my door and then came right in.

"Oh good," she said. "You're wearing the skirt. It's so much better than the dress."

"I know," I said. "Thanks for the fashion advice."

"No problem, little sis," she said, hugging me hard. She tossed a folded piece of paper on my bed. "For your autobiography."

"Thanks," I said. "It's not due till May."

"I know. I was just thinking last night about the contest while I was getting outfits for you to try on and basically realizing how awesome you are."

My whole face was spreading into a smile that had started somewhere in my stomach.

She went on. "But I didn't know when the next time would be that I would think you were annoying, so I thought I better write the letter right now."

We both giggled.

"Come on," she said. She was out the door and tramping down the stairs in her new green Doc Martens—a Christmas gift from Auntie Gina. I pressed her letter to my chest for a second before opening it up.

Dear Steffy,

I am really proud of you. I know you're totally going to win Chefs of Tomorrow. You are so much more patient and nice than I am. You are kinda like a stuffed animal. You are the best sister in the world. I like that you can cook, and I like that you are usually up for anything. You always really think about what people might like to eat and then you make it for them. I love your pasta, your burritos, your banana bread, and mostly anything that you make (maybe someday polenta!). Sometimes I wish I could be more like you.

Love,

Nina

The mascara that Nina had put on me was all over my fingers, and I had to go rinse off before going downstairs. In the kitchen, everyone was talking at the same time. Harry thought we should put the gnocchi in a Tupperware. Auntie Gina thought that we should leave them in the big blue-and-white dish that had been in the Sandolini family for years, for good luck. Dad said, What if that dish dropped or something? And Nina agreed with Harry and Dad. Everyone was all fussing over me and the contest, and I was wiping my cheeks every second. More mascara to wash off on my fingers.

In the end, Tupperware won. We drove downtown to Grasshopper Stadium. Auntie Gina and Dad found the table where you drop off your stuff, and I got number 19. There was a catch in my throat when Auntie Gina stepped back and let Dad fill out the paper. It didn't matter that I had said I was my own guardian—you still had to have a parent's signature when you signed in.

They had a band playing on the baseball field, and the contest was in the parking lot under these white tents. They had hot dogs and pizza and funnel cakes and raffle tickets to buy, and even games like throw the ring around the empty soda bottle to win a stuffed animal.

Joe Glorioso from school was there with his mom and dad, and Jean Sawyer, and even Mrs. Ashton.

"Steffany Sandolini," she said, squeezing my hand. "I've said it before and I'll say it again. Turning in the application for this contest instead of an outline? Creative thinking! And I will take you up on what you said that day: you are definitely writing about this in your autobiography. Got it?"

I nodded, and Mrs. Ashton gave me a hug. "Thank you for coming," I said. Wow. Even my English teacher (not even my favorite class) was here for me.

Lisa found us and she grabbed my hand, and we walked around and checked out all the entries. Something beefy. Some kind of shish kebab. Spaghetti. Fancy judges were going to taste all this. Family was different, because they were used to eating what you made. And they were usually hungry. What if the judges were so full when they got to mine, they thought it was gross?

We got seats up front by the judges' tables. Pretty soon Bob Sebuda—*the* Bob Sebuda from the channel 3 news—stepped onto the stage.

"Welcome, miniature Greensboro gourmets! I'm Bob Sebuda from channel 3 news, and we have here today over one hundred eager epicures between the ages of five and seventeen, all competing in three age categories for a spot in the Chefs of Tomorrow finals. Now, I've got twenty judges behind me who are *starving*!"

He said how they'd basically just be tasting and talking over the next few hours, how there were rides and games and snacks to buy, and how leftovers would go to charities all over Greensboro. He also said how Chefs of Tomorrow was sponsored by Elon University's Culinary Arts department.

"So here we go, ladies and gentlemen," he said. "Let the feeding begin!" And then the judges started coming around to all the food and taking it back to several long tables under a big tent.

They ate a whole lot and talked loudly into microphones, and you could barely understand them over the music. Sometimes people clapped. We just hung out and goofed around, and it was a good thing that Lisa was holding my hand hard when they got to number 19, because I thought I would fall out of my seat from watching so hard.

I could pick out lots of mmm-ing and nodding. I made out the words *sausage* and *flavor.* Then I thought I heard one of the lady judges say she'd never had gnocchi as good. Lisa's eyes lit up and her jaw dropped, and she kind of jumped up and down in her chair. When they got to my pie, there was lots of ooh-ing.

Then more and more and more and more and more eating. Just little bits of each entry. We took a walk around. Joe Glorioso found us and told us that a squirrel came right up onto their table and stole his hot dog bun. We had hot dogs and lemonades. When the sun started to go down and the sky got more orange, you could feel this big shift in the day because the grown-ups with the cups of beer started to laugh louder and dance harder. The only cup I saw Dad with all day was a pink lemonade cup.

It crept into my head that I hadn't seen any stashes of beer in our fridge in a while. Also creeping around inside me was that Mom and Helen didn't get to come to Chefs of Tomorrow after all, but there was so much else going on that I just didn't let myself dwell on it.

After the tasting portion was over, anyone could go up and exchange raffle tickets for samples of the entries while the judges went off and decided on the winners. Lisa and Nina and I each had a lemon cupcake with vanilla frosting and sprinkles. That person's main course was lemon chicken. Me and Lisa giggled that she had suggested that to me a month back.

Finally, it was getting time to announce the winners. There were fifty kids in my age group. That meant there was a ten percent chance I'd be in the final five.

"I don't think I'm going to win," I whispered to Lisa as we walked past beautiful platters of meats, vegetables, pastas, and stir-frys.

"Oh hush, Steffany."

The music got turned down finally, and Bob Sebuda spoke into the microphone again.

"From here," he said, "the finalists whose names I am about to announce will have the next two and a half months to perfect their dishes. Then, on June fifteenth, they will join us to prepare their meals in a live televised broadcast."

Auntie Gina squeezed my hand, and Lisa said, "Oh my gosh, oh my gosh, oh my gosh."

Bob continued. "It's been tough," he said, "but we have narrowed it down to five finalists in each of the three age groups. The following fifteen fabulous foodies will compete for slots on the menu at Greensboro's own farm-to-table fine dining establishment Lucky Thirty-Two, and a cash award of three thousand dollars. Our second-place winners will receive cooking lessons at Elon University. The folks at Elon will also see to it that leftovers from today's contest are donated to charities all across our city, so let's give them a big hand right now for their support of balanced meals for all." The audience whooted and hollered for a few seconds and then Bob quieted people down.

First he announced the winners in the family category, where little kids cooked something with help from a parent. Then nine-to-twelve. He said that for some reason nine-to-twelve was the hardest one because that was where the highest quality of cooking came from. Lisa grabbed me around my waist. Nina squeezed my arm, and Auntie Gina held both my hands. Dad stood right by her, showing me his crossed fingers.

Bob Sebuda called out, "In the nine-to-twelve category:

number twelve, traditional turkey dinner and cranberry pumpkin pie! Number forty-nine, caramel beef stew with vegetables and caramel apples! Number three, barbecued catfish and king cake! Number eighteen, Asian noodle stir-fry and vanilla soy cookies!"

Nina put her hand on my shoulder, Lisa held my waist tighter, and Auntie Gina squeezed my hands harder. Dad lifted one finger and nodded at me.

"And number nineteen, potato gnocchi and yam-pecan pie!"

Chef of Today

I am pretty sure I smiled while I slept all that night.

A Thing of Pizza Dough

I felt bad that it took me becoming a finalist—to have that feeling inside of me—for me to decide to crawl into my closet past balled-up pants and sock clumps to find the cake magazines that I'd shoved in there before Christmas. Laundry was on the bottom of the list at home, now that Dad was in charge. But somehow it worked out in the mornings—there were always clean things around somewhere to put on for the day.

I flipped through the pages of a magazine called *The Knot*, and with each cake photo, I got more panicked. Hopefully Auntie Gina didn't really want me to make her a cake in the shape of a cruise ship or a glass slipper. I hoped she had given me the magazines to have something to give and not because she had one of these in mind.

For the first time, maybe, it felt like living apart from Auntie Gina was a good thing. I had put the magazines in my closet and hated her for a while, but I didn't have to see her every day and didn't have to hide that from her. She always said I needed to express myself more. Like, if I was mad at anyone, they'd never know because if I showed it, then they'd get mad at *me* and that's what I didn't want to happen. And if you got mad at magazines and not at a person, maybe it was better because I wasn't mad anymore, and Auntie Gina didn't even ever have to know and feel mad or bad.

I flipped through the second magazine, *Bridal Guide*. More crazy but cool pictures. Giant and elaborate layer cakes full of multicolored flowers. A cake that looked like presents stacked on top of each other. The more I looked, the more I knew I was just going to do a simple yet elegant layer cake.

But then there were the old Italian dessert recipes, like pizza frittas, that might be good to make for the wedding, too.

It was Sunday morning, the very next day after the Chefs of Tomorrow semifinals, and Nina was at a special dance practice for anyone in her studio auditioning for Charlotte Rep, and Dad had gotten a job painting a new office building, and it was just me for a few hours.

I went downstairs, and I opened my mom's cookbook and flipped through for more dessert ideas. I found the pizza frittas paper again and read it through. Easy enough. Just frying dough, basically. Then I came across a yellowy piece of crinkled paper that said "S's and O's—Italian Wedding Cookies."

Oh my gosh, I remembered these. Somewhere, sometime so long ago, I remembered a platter of them: small puffy cookies with pink icing on the ones shaped like an *S* and white icing on the ones shaped like an *O*. And my grandma, my mom and Auntie Gina's mom, in a dark-blue dress and an apron and glasses and hair in a bun. The shaky handwriting was probably hers, my grandma's, because it didn't match the recipes my mom had written.

There were so many things I could do for Auntie Gina's wedding. I wanted to make her the best thing that she and Harry wanted though. I knew Harry was a carrot cake freak, but not everyone liked carrot cake. And Auntie Gina had given me these magazines to give me an idea of what she might want. I figured I'd maybe do a batch of either pizza frittas or S's and O's, for tradition, and a cake with a bunch of layers of different flavors.

Layer cakes always made me think of commercials where the daughter licked frosting off her mom's finger. But I had always licked frosting off Auntie Gina's finger. I could never see myself licking frosting off Dad's finger, I didn't think.

Maybe I was too old for licking frosting off someone's finger anyway, whether it was a mom or an aunt or a dad. Since Dad had come, I had been getting used to giving myself my own cooking tips, deciding on my own what was for dinner, licking frosting off my own fingers.

A few days after I won, on Wednesday after school, Dad took me on the bus to the Extra Ingredient, and he let me spend twenty dollars on anything I wanted because he said it was payday.

We walked down the kitchen utensil aisle slowly, because I wanted to get a look at everything they had. Stainless steel was the theme, and it was all beautiful stuff. Power blenders and cookie cutters and wire whisks and pie tins and anything you could ever think of for your kitchen.

"I'm selfishly hoping you'll do some practice cakes for your aunt's wedding, you know," he said.

I giggled and could feel my face going hot. I just nodded. It was the first time me and Dad had gone alone together somewhere since I could ever remember. We didn't have enough for the power blender itself, but I got these way-cool smoothie cups and another cake pan.

Since it was just a few streets over, we stopped off at the Harris Teeter because I wanted to get a thing of pizza dough. The pizza frittas recipe from my mom's cookbook had been bouncing around in my head, and I wanted to try it.

On the way home on the bus, with all our bags at our

feet, I thought about my afternoon out with my dad. Having him all to myself, it was like I got to see him up close. And he got to see me, too. I noticed that we both stare out windows and that we both chose fruity gum over mint. We were more alike than I'd thought.

Shaking on the Sugar

Pizza frittas made me have a whole new appreciation for pizza dough. It's the exact same dough. If you take it and bake it with sauce and cheese and meat on it, it's a savory main course. If you take it and fry it and put sugar all over it, it's a sweet dessert. I was jumping out of my skin to bring pizza frittas to Mom. Maybe she'd remember her own mom. And maybe more.

Jean Sawyer was waiting after church wearing jeans and a sweatshirt. She was usually so much more dressed up, but then we got to the Place and I didn't think about it anymore. I couldn't wait to give Mom the frittas.

She ate two and went for a third, and Helen said she

thought that was plenty. (Auntie Gina would have said, "But she's Italian—she can *always* have more.") I asked if we could offer some to the others because they were all staring. Helen said yes.

"Mom," I said, "you remember making these? Pizza frittas?"

She squinted while she wiped her mouth.

"You know," I said, "you take pizza dough and break it into balls and fry it up? Then sprinkle on sugar?"

Nina chewed at her thumbnail.

Mom shook her head. "I don't know, honey. I can't . . . I can't picture it."

We had to leave it there because more and more people were coming over for frittas.

In Greensboro, April can be funny. The city is in bloom, but the sky can stay gray for a week solid, and we were having a cloudy week like that. But having the frittas at the Place dusted off some of the gloom. And all right. Maybe Mom wouldn't remember stuff on every single visit that we brought snacks, but maybe on some visits she would. I decided I would bring something every week to increase the chances.

Nina told Mom that I was a finalist in the Bob Sebuda contest. And I told Mom that Nina was trying out for Charlotte Rep. There were too many things that I hoped would happen, and I wanted to erase some of them so I didn't get disappointed.

I put my hand by Mom's hand, and we just both looked down together. She didn't have the thick fingers that me and Auntie Gina had. Hers were slender and beautiful. The nails were all perfectly groomed and not jagged and bitten down, like Nina's. Mom's hands could jump all over a piano, and according to Auntie Gina, she used to make the best pasta in the world. I put her finger to my lips, and I kissed it.

"Good to spend time with your mom, huh?" said Jean when we were all piled into the car.

"Yeah," I said. Nina nodded.

"Steffy, your homemade meals have been a hit over there. Not just with your mom, either."

"Yeah," I said. I was kind of disappointed that Mom didn't remember anything this time though. Nina and Jean started talking about how spring was taking forever to officially just come, and I was in the backseat holding on to a thought and not wanting to let it go, like not wanting to let go of Mom's hand. I couldn't work out why it was so important to be remembered. Why it was so big to be talked about and to have people know about you and listen to things about you and want to know more things about you. If I could have crawled into the reason for wanting Mom to remember me, for wanting Dad to keep noticing, I would have stayed there forever to just know it and know it and know it.

The Donation Pie

There were a million things that were happening. Farthest off: Mom's birthday, July 1. Closer was Harry and Gina's wedding, June 22. Even closer was Chefs of Tomorrow, June 15. And first was my autobiography assignment, which was due May 28.

It was the last Saturday in April, and so I had a month to finish it. I had my letter from Nina, and as I rode my bike to St. Theresa's that morning, I wondered if I might gather more letters. I wondered if that would be okay with Mrs. Ashton.

Spring weather that had taken so long to officially come had slipped through our fingers like long spaghettis slip off your fork, and now it was just plain old hot. I was now a robot at making gnocchi, and I'd brought batches to school for Principal Schmitz-Brady, to Gina and Harry's for Harry's birthday, and to the Place for all the residents in the rec room. Mom hadn't come up with any memories that day, but she had eaten three helpings.

With a yam-pecan pie in my bike basket, I pulled up right outside the church. I had baked a couple practice pies, and I thought I'd donate the too-sticky one to the soup kitchen. It was bona fide hot outside, and as I put the kickstand down, I noticed how sweaty I was.

I went into the church and handed over the pie to the receptionist. I hoped it hadn't gotten as soggy as I had from the humidity. After taking the pie and thanking me, she went back to flipping through a stack of papers.

Church was still and empty inside. And cool. Oh, it felt so good in there—not as cold as the Harris Teeter feels, especially in the frozen-foods aisle, but better than outside.

I hadn't come over to the church just because I was being a good citizen and donating the pie. But it was smart to have an official reason to come, and the pie was a perfect excuse. I glanced toward the basement steps. I pretended like there was suddenly an important thing that I had to go down there for, and I walked, like a person with an important reason would, right over and started going down. With each stair, I covered my nose and mouth with my shirt to block out the cigarette smoke.

There was this girl standing up in front of everyone. I saw Dad and Carol in their regular seats. The guy with the ponytail from last time was in the front row. I crouched down in the middle of the stairway where I could see everything pretty good and tried to be invisible.

"I was fourteen when I had the baby," the girl said. She said she had it in the hospital and her mom didn't show up and her boyfriend didn't show up and it was a girl and they took it right after it was born to give it away but then she started to feel all bad and started partying, she said, just like her mom. She said it was all around the house. It got so bad she stopped going to high school and then stopped doing anything, it got so bad.

The more she talked, the more I liked her, with her long hair and glasses. She talked all the way up to being twenty-three and living with her boyfriend downtown, and she said it got worse and worse. She said she had another baby, a boy, that was one pound and died. She said she hadn't seen her mom in over ten years, but she's thinking of trying to find her now. And she said the best thing she ever did was give up that first baby, because she knew she couldn't take care of it the way that she thought she should.

My stomach started hurting. I felt like I was about to get in trouble, like I did something really wrong. Like by knowing these things, by sneaking down there, everything was too scary and real. This wasn't TV or reading something online. This was right in front of me.

I thought of all the pieces of Dad that I was putting together since he came back. Him telling us about being at the ocean and feeling like the only person in the world and those big, scary waves. I thought about him deciding to move to California. Him telling Carol about all the eyes on him in Greensboro. But even though there were eyes, maybe he came back because he thought he could take care of us now the way that he thought he should.

I tiptoed upstairs, where the faint smell of incense filled the sanctuary. The church was just as quiet as it had been before I went down—there were only a few old ladies doing rosaries—but there was so much jumbling around inside of me that I felt like it was so loud they could hear.

I didn't want to know about what the girl was saying, but at the same time I did want to know. Nina was going to be fourteen this summer, exactly that girl's age when she had her first baby. And I was only three years from fourteen, but I felt one million years from her story. I wondered what Dad's story was about, and I really wondered what my story someday would be.

The Cream-Puff Flash

We brought cream puffs to Mom's the next day, and we got all messy eating them. I sat right by Mom with our arms around each other and told her about the contest again, how the finals were coming up in June. Nina talked about Charlotte Rep auditions, too. And I even told her that Dad was doing good, painting a big building downtown.

"Tell me more about James," said Mom. Nina's eyes shot over to mine, and she shook her head.

"Good, Mom, you knew that his name is James. He's . . . pretty good," I said. We couldn't tell her about James because we didn't really have much to tell.

"How is *my* dad?" asked Mom.

"He died a while back," said Nina. "Maybe, like, eight or nine years ago."

Mom's eyes got full, and me and Nina hugged her more. "My dad's mad at me," Mom said. I took one of her hands, and Nina took the other.

"No," said Nina. "Nobody's mad at you, Mom."

Helen said sometimes a memory will flash to a TBI person that will feel so close but that will be something that happened years and years and years ago, and they can't figure out the difference. I laid my head on Mom's shoulder and rubbed her hand.

I couldn't stop thinking about the girl downstairs at church and those two babies. Even though they were sad memories, she talked about them at the meeting, and it seemed to make her feel better. It made me mad at God that he would take away someone's memories—or jumble them around—all the little things that made up who they were. I was also mad at the cream puffs, because I wondered if they made Mom remember something bad about her dad.

Maybe bringing food to Mom was a bad idea. How could I know what memories were connected to what foods? I definitely didn't want to come visit our mom and make her upset.

Later that night, I called Lisa.

"I need your talkies," I said. There was a pause.

"My lunar-talkies? What are you up to, Steffany Sandolini?"

I didn't tell her everything on the phone because it was almost time for bed, but she agreed to bring them.

The following morning before advisory group, Lisa and I secretly transferred her lunar-talkies from her backpack to mine. It wasn't a secret to have them at school, but it was secret what we were going to do with them.

"Thanks," I said.

"Ten-four, Houston," she said.

If Dad was a little bit slow to tell us more stuff about himself, I was going to keep trying to find out my own way.

Sauce and Stew Meat and Down the Stairs

After going down and watching the meeting once, the second time was easier. I felt freer, but also knew that I had to be so careful and not make a sound. If Dad saw me, I didn't know what I'd do. But I was just too curious not to go back, and with Nina at all these extra practices for the Charlotte Rep tryouts, I was by myself a lot of Saturdays.

After handing over the Tupperware of leftover sauce and stew meat to the receptionist for the soup kitchen, I snuck downstairs.

Carol told everyone about when she was married and had all these kids, and she never knew they were really there. How they still hated her, some of them. How she could never go back and do the right things but how she was trying to now. How she thought about them all every day and how she hated herself some days. "But I don't hate myself enough to go back," she said. She smoked and smoked while she talked. She said she was sober for nineteen years. From the first meeting I watched, I knew that meant she hadn't been doing drugs or drinking.

There were parts of her story where you just couldn't believe she was saying it out loud to people—things about leaving her twin babies and her four-year-old alone all night, about stealing money. Things a person wouldn't ever want anyone to know about. She said the only thing she was glad about was that none of the babies died. And that someday maybe they'd forgive her. She said she didn't care if it didn't happen until after she was dead, as long as someday they did.

I had the same sick feeling when I left as I had after the first meeting. Like I was going to get in trouble for hearing these things, like hearing them right there in that same room with a person that I ate Thanksgiving dinner with was so much scarier than hearing something like that in a movie or on TV. Carol was real and this was her story, not like an actor playing a part.

This was the grown-up world that I saw on Dad's face the morning after Chrismtas. Being on this stair was being in that world—a different Greensboro that I never knew about.

I had to keep coming back until I heard Dad's story.

Later that afternoon when Nina was at Denise's and Dad was still not home from "work" (or "choir practice"), I went out front with one of the lunar-talkies. Lisa had said the batteries inside were new, and so I turned it to On and shoved it right inside the overgrown bushes behind the card table.

The Berries Keep Spinning and Spinning

The following Saturday, Dad wasn't going down to his meeting. He didn't tell me that, of course, but I knew it because instead he was taking Nina and Denise to try out for Charlotte Rep. His car deal hadn't happened yet, so they were taking the bus. I'd have been nervous about what to say to him during the two hours to Charlotte, but I knew Nina'd be fine. I couldn't get over that Dad was actually going to bring them all the way down there, wait while they auditioned, and then bring them back. Like an actual dad would do.

"I don't think I'm gonna get in," said Nina.

"Nina," said Denise, "think positive."

I was in the kitchen adding strawberries to the blender. I was kind of jumpy around Dad, because when you spy on people and then you see them normally, you feel like any second you're gonna get caught, and I wanted to keep spying. He stood by the door, fumbling around with his keys, waiting for Nina to put the rest of her stuff in her dance bag.

"I didn't think I would become a finalist in the cooking thing," I said, pouring milk into the blender.

"Oh, that was a cinch, Steffany. You have this totally unique talent."

"Dance is unique," I said.

"Not really," Nina said. I looked at Nina in her sweats and tank top, her hair in a bun, and she looked back. I knew I would never, ever be able to dance and maybe she knew she'd never want to cook, but we understood each other so perfectly right then.

I pushed Puree on the blender, and strawberries smashed to the side and milk shot up to the lid and ice popped around on top of the silvery blades. As they were about to walk out, I handed them each a smoothie.

"Oh my gosh, Steffy, yum! Where'd you get these cute cups?" asked Nina.

"The Extra Ingredient. Two for five dollars." I glanced at Dad, who gave me a thumbs-up. They said they loved the smoothies, and I said they were really easy, just strawberries, yogurt, and a little ice and apple juice in the blender. You could actually pop in any kind of fruit you wanted. Bananas, strawberries, blueberries, whatever sounded best to you.

Each time I added another ingredient, the smoothie changed and got better and more flavorful. While it blended, something became obvious to me: Nina, my mom, my dad, Auntie Gina—of course I would ask all of them for letters for my autobiography assignment.

It was due in two and a half weeks. Mrs. Ashton had given us lots of writing time in class lately, but all I did was put all the recipes that I'd made this year in an order. I wasn't sure how I was going to make that into an autobiography, but that's what kept feeling right.

At about noon, Auntie Gina came and got me, and we went to a few wedding dress places. It'd been a while since I had seen her and there was a big rush of wanting to cry for a second, but then there was all the stuff to tell her about and catch her up on. I was relieved to have her all to myself for the afternoon. I didn't even have to finish explaining about the autobiography project and the letter.

"I remember writing Nina's for her," she said. "When do you need it by?" she asked.

"It's due in, like, three weeks," I said.

"Well, if it isn't Last-Minute Lucy," she said.

"I know," I said. "But can you do it?"

"Steffy," she said, "it's not even a question."

When she put on a dress that had this purple sash thing

and white flowers around the neck, we both stopped talking.

"Oh my gosh," I said. "That's it."

"You think?" she said. And then both of us were crying and laughing as we looked at her reflection in the big mirror. Even though she was still my auntie Gina (sometimes she felt more like my mom), she was getting married, and I was betting it'd feel like she was even farther away from me after the wedding than it had felt since my dad came back.

"Steffy, you know that I went shopping with your mom when she got her wedding dress," she said.

"No," I said. I sat down and played with the ruffle on the cushy footrest thing that was in the big dressing room.

"Yeah," she said. "I remember that day."

She lifted her hair all on top of her head and watched herself in the mirror as she turned her head to one side.

"She was so excited to marry your daddy."

I couldn't look at Auntie Gina while she told me this. But I wanted to hear it so, so bad.

"Nobody else was that excited, though."

I had to look up.

"Not because of your dad, honey. We all loved James—we really did."

She turned to the side and held in her stomach. Then she let it out.

"They were just both really young, and your mom didn't even know what she wanted to *do* with herself yet. Everyone said she was gonna go get her degree in culinary arts or music. And she never did."

She gathered the skirt part of the dress in her hands and came over and sat down on the other fancy footrest thing and played with the ruffle.

After a minute she said, "I used to think that if I ever decided to get married, she'd come with me to do this."

I nodded and thought of Nina.

"Yeah," she said. "I remember that day. I remember so many days." She got up and turned around. "Unbutton me?"

I stood behind her and started unlooping the satiny buttons that lined the back of the dress like a row of candy mints.

"You know that when you were a baby, your mom used to cook with you."

"Yeah," I said, "I think I kind of knew that. You've said that before. What did she cook?"

"I remember her in the kitchen holding you on her hip, and she would be stirring sauce with her other hand. And when you got a little bigger, you were like her third arm, and you would dump in sugar and sprinkle in salt and whisk stuff. Nina never wanted to do any of that. But you, I mean, come on—your first words were 'wire whisk.'"

"What?" I asked.

"Yes!"

We started laughing. "I never told you that, Steffy?" she said. "Oh my gosh, I'm so sorry. Isn't that funny? I didn't even remember that until just now. I guess no one ever told you because . . . because everything changed."

We were quiet on the way to the Harris Teeter. Tomorrow was Mother's Day, and we were stopping to get flowers to bring Mom. A dark feeling snuck up on me every year around Mother's Day. Whenever I gave her those flowers, I worried that she would feel bad, that it would hurt her to be reminded that she was a mom and that she was supposed to be doing mom things instead of doing word searches and sitting around and playing the piano all day. But Auntie Gina always insisted.

Back in the car on the way home, Auntie Gina was telling me how people would have to make alterations to her dress, and she'd go back and pick it up when it was ready. I was half listening and half thinking about smoothies and mixing in more fruit. How the blade at the bottom of the blender zipped around and around so fast, and how no matter how many times I went over it and over it and over it in my head, no matter how many dishes I brought for Mom, no matter how many bouquets I bought her on Mother's Day—my mom had lived at the Place since I could remember, and she would probably live at the Place for a long, long time.

Breakfast for Dinner

Nina had spent the night at Denise's when they got back from tryouts, and because they were so exhausted, she didn't come to the Place on Sunday. I had hoped Nina would call me and tell me how it went, but I'd have to wait until she got home. I mean, I hadn't told her to call me or anything. They would find out if they made it in a couple weeks, Dad said. I hoped they'd both make it. But the more things I was hoping for, the more nervous I got about everything. I was hoping for things for other people, but underneath I was also thinking about the Chefs of Tomorrow finals that were only a month away now.

Jean Sawyer just stared straight ahead the whole way to Mom's. I couldn't tell if we were quiet because Nina wasn't there, or if we were quiet just because. But there was something different about Jean, like she was really busy in her head, thinking about something. Anyway, it gave me time to think about how to ask Mom about the letter.

She was on the couch with the newspaper when we got there. When she saw me, she put it down and smiled and glanced at Helen, who told her I was her daughter. "Happy Mother's Day, Mom," I said. I handed off the bouquet of yellow and white daisies to Helen, and she said she'd go get a vase. I leaned down and hugged and kissed Mom. So we wouldn't have time to think about Mother's Day, I got right to business and blurted it all out, how I had to write a biographical letter to myself for school.

"There's also this parent letter thing," I said. "Mrs. Ashton wants us to have our parent or guardian write a letter to us about who they think we are."

"Who they think you are," Mom said. A couple seconds went by.

"Could you maybe write it?" I asked. "For me?"

She sighed. Then smiled really big. "I could," she said. "I could try."

"Yeah, just try," I said. "I could even help you. If you want."

Once the flowers were in a vase on a little side table nearby, Helen brought a pencil and a notebook and gave it to Mom. I scooted closer to her, and we figured out that she'd jot things down so she wouldn't forget during the week. Helen said she and my mom could write down details on Sundays after me and Nina visited. There were two Sundays left after this one, before it was due. So Mom had time to write her letter based on the details she got down during each of our visits instead of just trying to remember it all.

I told her all about Chefs of Tomorrow again, how I was in fifth grade, how my best friend was Lisa Rudder. That we lived with Dad. Then I didn't know what else to say. It was hard for me to come up with things that would go good in a letter *to* me about who *she* thought I was. It was kind of giving me a headache. But I talked about how I loved to make breakfast every morning, how I pretty much liked school, and how Lisa wanted to be an astronaut but was also really good at helping me come up with cooking ideas and we might go into business making astronaut desserts.

I liked this, having her write it down. Maybe she'd remember us more now that she was going to start writing things down every week. It was like writing down a recipe. Like, I made chocolate chip banana bread a lot. Maybe once a month or something. But I never remembered exactly how much sugar I was supposed to put in. I always had to look at the recipe. And Mom was writing down all the ingredients of me so she could go back and remember. Plus, asking her to write the letter wasn't as scary as I thought it'd be.

Now there was only one more person to ask.

That evening, I made a greasy-spoon dinner of eggs, bacon, and pancakes. I had been too nervous about asking for those darn letters to think about cooking an actual *dinner* dinner.

"So," Dad said once we were all seated at the table, "it looks like this little hatchback is gonna be ours soon." He opened his phone and showed us another photo of that same small, red car that he talked about before.

"Sweet," said Nina.

"I'm gonna have to teach you to drive in a couple years, and then you, Steffy. Plus, I want to be able to pick you guys up and take you where you need to go."

It was the first time ever that Dad actually said something about what was going to happen later on with us, like, in the future. It gave me goose bumps.

Then Nina said two big words.

"Thank you."

Dad nodded before taking a slurp of coffee. Something invisible in me stretched to hug him from my chair. Then I told him all about the autobiography project.

"I kind of decided to go for lots of letters instead of one, well, just because of how things are."

Dad and I locked eyes for a second.

"I'm picking up Mom's letter in a couple weeks. And Auntie Gina's writing me one. And Nina wrote me one, too." I took a breath. "And I want one more."

The Good News Potpie Meal

The following Thursday in English class Mrs. Ashton just gave us time to write and work on our autobiographies. I had less than two weeks to get it all done. I was trying to put together all the stories that Auntie Gina had told me about from when I was little.

Harry and Auntie Gina had invited everyone over for dinner that night. They had thrown stuff that they had around into a kind of potpie—ham, cheese, mushrooms, sprouts, and red peppers were inside, and then there was this biscuity and delicious thing around the outside. They served it with garlicky potato wedges and sweet tea, and it was perfect. We were all sitting around Auntie Gina's big table. Dad too.

He was telling Harry that his boss had sold him our new maroon Honda. Auntie Gina was telling me to boil the asparagus before you put it in the potpie to make sure it was well done and not hard. I was asking her how she could figure out what things to put together that would taste good in a Kitchen Sink kind of meal when Nina's cell phone rang.

"It's Charlotte Rep," she said, looking at the number that came up. "They're calling me! I thought they were gonna call Dad or something. And I didn't know we were gonna find out this quick." She pleaded with Auntie Gina for permission to answer it during dinner, and Auntie Gina said, "Oh please, girl, of course. Hurry!" Nina got up and ran into the living room with her phone. At the table, we all stared at each other, and no one breathed. For a minute maybe we just heard Nina saying, "Yes" and "Okay," and then she said, "Oh good." Auntie squeezed my hand.

"I got in!" Nina yelled as she ran back to the table. I screamed. Auntie Gina jumped out of her seat and went to hug Nina. Everybody was up and hugging her, and she was wiping her eyes.

"They want me there early, Auntie Gina. They said I was in the top five and could I come early for them to train me to be a team leader. Oh my God," she said. "I can't believe it." She took a tissue from Harry. "Can I go call Denise, Auntie Gina? Please?"

She said yes, and Nina ran into the living room.

Auntie Gina said she guessed Dad could call our school and explain how Nina had been singled out in the top five and ask if she could leave school early. It got decided that Nina would come back up here for Mom's birthday—Dad even said he'd drive down to get her. And Harry said that we'd all go down and watch her performances at the end of the summer and then bring her back up to Greensboro together. Auntie Gina and Dad were easier with each other, like they were better friends now or something.

On that night I loved how my family was, all of us talking at the same time about Nina, making these plans together about the things that we'd do. I glanced at Dad, who was bringing dishes to Auntie Gina at the sink, and imagined the two of us together all summer while Nina was in Charlotte. I would cook, he would read the paper, we would eat Snickers bars.

Harry came and gave me a squeeze and whispered, "Just about a month away for you, huh?" We were celebrating my sister, but he was also thinking about me and Chefs of Tomorrow. I was letting myself like him again, when I had been so mad that he was taking Auntie Gina away. She was our aunt, after all, not our mom. We belonged to her sister. And to Dad.

When Nina got off the phone with Denise, I ran up to her.

"Denise got in!" she said.

"And you got in," I said. "Top five."

"Yeah," she said, wrinkling her nose. I hadn't noticed the little freckles she had on her cheeks in a long time. She looked younger than thirteen right then, and she put her arms around my neck and I put my arms around her waist and we hugged. I wondered what you thought of your sister when you were little compared to what you thought of your sister when you grew up, and I hoped I'd always feel like I did right then.

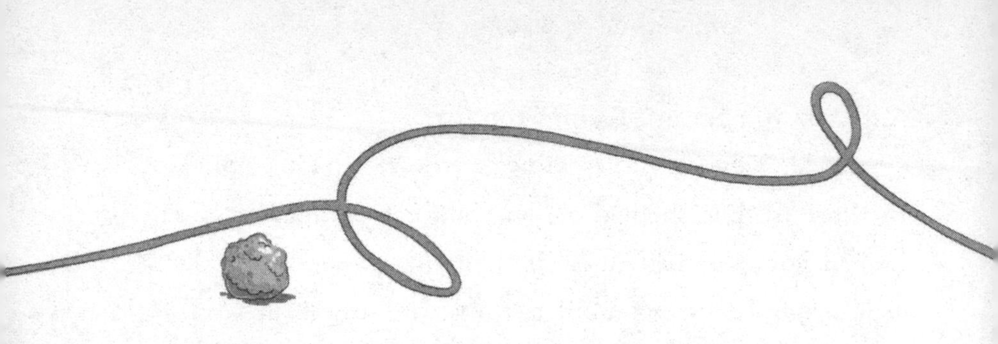

Jeannie Beannie's Lemon Bars

On Sunday, Jean Sawyer wasn't waiting for us at church. Nina called Dad's cell. No answer. We waited a few minutes. The receptionist called Jean's house. No answer. Nina called Auntie Gina at work.

"Hey," said Nina. "We're at church waiting for Jean but she's not —"

She stopped. "What?"

I could feel something wrong.

"Oh no," said Nina, sitting down on the bench right there outside the office. The receptionist and I looked at each other. "Oh my God," Nina said. She looked at me. "I will," she said. "Bye."

"What?" I asked when she had ended the call.

"Jean got really sick again."

"Is she okay?"

"No, Steffy," said Nina. "She's not."

I heard the receptionist say, "Oh dear."

Nina turned to her and said, "My aunt said she was in the hospital for a few days and she just . . ." Nina sighed. "We didn't even know."

"Know what?" I asked.

"That she was even in the hospital."

"Is she better?"

"Steffy," said Nina, "she died."

Oh my gosh.

Nina and the receptionist were talking for a minute. I just stared at the spot I last remembered Jean Sawyer in the vestibule. It was magic. She disappeared from the Earth when she was *just there* before, talking, breathing, laughing. I wondered where she was and what she was doing. I wanted to thank her again for helping us, because I never really thanked her enough.

Me and Nina didn't get to go see Mom that day, so Auntie Gina figured out with her work that she'd go in late the next day, Monday, and after school, the three of us would go visit Mom special.

That night I went through the old cookbook. I couldn't remember what it was, but there was one recipe in there that made me think of Jean Sawyer. I flipped and flipped through the pages and pages of recipes, some so old they felt like tissue paper, and I was extra careful. Scraps of notebook paper shoved in, index cards, newspaper clippings with recipes for something with chicken or pork chops. And then, finally: Jeannie Beannie's Lemon Bars.

I called Auntie Gina and asked her if we could make lemon bars with Mom tomorrow, and she said yes, as long as Helen said okay. She said she'd call her and ask. I told her all the ingredients over the phone.

It was almost eight thirty and time to get ready for bed, but I baked a crust anyway. The recipe was simple—just flour, butter, water, and salt. And this kind of dough was so easy to knead compared with pasta dough because the butter made it real squishy and pliable.

The next day after school, Nina skipped dance, and Auntie Gina came and got us special to go over to the Place. She had everything for the bars, plus my crust. While Mom and Auntie Gina sat and talked in the rec room for a while, me and Nina followed Helen back through hallway D, and then down another winding hallway, and then through the dining hall and into the big kitchen in the back.

"Have at it, ladies," she said. "The crew'll start dinner in about an hour. You think you have enough time?" We said yes. Wow. Baking in a giant kitchen where they made meals for big, huge crowds of people. Nina was unloading our lemon bar stuff onto the long marble counter, and I found mixing bowls and utensils in the many cabinets and drawers. I wondered what the Chefs of Tomorrow finals would be like and if I would be in a kitchen this big.

We started to mix together the lemon filling—it actually turned out to be pretty easy—and it smelled so good. We preheated the oven. Me and Nina didn't talk that much. The ceilings were so high in there, and it almost felt like church and we should be quiet. Plus, all I wanted to do was bake. We were just about to pour the filling into the crust when Mom and Auntie Gina came in.

"Do you want to help?" I asked.

Mom came around to the other side of the counter, and as I poured, she turned the pan around to get it evenly in there. It was a small thing that we did together in the kitchen, me and my mom, but it was the first time baking with her, ever, that I could remember.

"Oh, that smells good," said Auntie Gina.

Nina and I washed the dishes in silence while Mom and Auntie Gina sat on some stools nearby and talked quietly. The smell of sweet lemon and warm crust filled the air. Over the running water and the clank of mixing bowls and measuring cups, I could tell that Mom and Auntie Gina were talking about real things and not chitchatting.

"My dad died eight or nine years ago," I could hear Mom saying when we had turned off the water and were drying the dishes.

"Nine," said Auntie Gina.

"But how long ago did *their* daddy die?" Mom pointed to me and Nina, prying into us with her eyes.

"Mom," I said, "he didn't."

She nodded her head slowly. "Well, where's he been?"

Nobody knew how to answer that one. I wondered how many times Auntie Gina had tried. She did again today:

"James is having a hard time."

"Me too," said Mom. Auntie Gina took Mom's hand.

"Steffy," said Auntie Gina, "you and Nina go and tell Helen that the bars are almost ready and ask if it's okay to share with everyone, okay?"

As me and Nina walked back down hallway D, I thought about how baking with Mom was something that was only in stories about me that Auntie Gina told. Like how some of the Grandpa Falcon memories were only in pictures. And how the time we spent actually living with Jean Sawyer for a little while was something that I knew happened, but I was too little to really remember. It must have been a big deal for her to have these two kids actually live with her in her house, and I couldn't even tell one thing about it.

Later, when me and Nina were lifting Jeannie Beannie's Lemon Bars out of the pan with spatulas, I thought about how Jean Sawyer may have known me better than I ever realized. How all the things that she might have remembered about me were now gone with her. How selfish and mean it was for me to think of her like that now that she had died. How I wished I had talked to her more when she was alive; how I wished I had not been so shy.

Keep Cooking, Hot Stuff

We brought the lemon bars to the family party (what else do you call it—there's food and laughter and people hugging) after Jean Sawyer's funeral. It was weird to think of Jean Sawyer having a mom and a dad and brothers and sisters and nieces and nephews, and it made me feel nervous and out of place there, to think that she was closer to all of them than she was to me. But she was still my Jean Sawyer, who baked better than me, who saw us every Sunday, who knew me from when I was a baby.

Jean Sawyer's mom and dad sat in wheelchairs side by side holding hands, and you could just tell those were two of the best people in the world. Someone got everyone's attention, and her dad told us all how grateful they were that we came and celebrated Jeannie. How they knew she was resting peacefully and that they could let her go.

After the speech, when everyone at the party was talking again and there was even lots of laughter, I saw Dad go up and kneel by Jean's parents and talk to them a lot. I got this tight feeling in my chest, thinking, should I go talk to them too? No, I wouldn't. I wouldn't know what to say. And then somehow, something was telling me just go, just go, and then I was going over there and kneeling down, just like I saw my dad do.

"Hi there, missy," said Jean's dad.

"Hi," I said. "We made lemon bars in honor of Jean."

"Yes, I saw that. Thank you," said Jean's mom.

"We . . . loved Jean," I said.

The dad nodded and put his hand on my head, and said, "Just keep cooking, hot stuff."

I was thinking about what church says about how if you were good, you get to go to heaven when you die. But Lisa says there is no heaven. She says you come back to Earth as a puppy or another person and have another life. I don't think I'd like that, being a puppy. Lisa says that even though you die, you keep getting to come back to live more and more. I sent off a little message to wherever Jean Sawyer was and told her hi. I pretended like she said hi back. I had never known anyone who'd died before, and I decided that in my version of dying, you could talk to the person and they could hear you. I only wished they could talk back.

That night I was pulling the covers up over me and lying down when this crashing, staticky sound came from my dresser. The lunar-talkie.

"Oh my gosh," I said out loud, and bounded off my bed.

". . . No, I didn't think you would have," said Dad's voice. Then a sound like *shhhhhhhhh* . . . and then silence. And then another *shhhhhhhhh* noise. Then more talking. It was Carol.

"But you're not the first person to say something like that."

"It's all of it hitting you, you know?" Dad said. "I'd betrayed everyone. I'd missed holidays, birthdays, funerals—my uncle died, and I didn't even know it."

Shhhhhhhhh.

". . . up everything. And that morning," he said, "it was so quiet. There were no waves."

Shhhhhhhhh. More of that static. And then nothing. Darn it. It sounded like it even switched off somehow. I pressed and pressed On, and nothing. There was that same speeding-up feeling in me from when I got the idea to bring polenta to Mom. My motor was running and I flew downstairs in my T-shirt and sweats as fast as I could. The kitchen was totally dark and I left the lights off, and I climbed as carefully as I could up onto the counter by the sink. Dad had cracked the kitchen window and there was a breeze coming in, making the curtains billow out into my face a little bit.

From out front I heard Carol coughing. Then two clicks of her cigarette lighter.

"In the actual sand," Dad said. "I don't know about the night before. But there I was, stretched out in Santa Monica. It hits you in the morning, always. You come crashing down. I'd made bad choices, I'd betrayed everyone in my life who cared anything about me. I'd stood in front of the world and screwed up."

"Yes, sir," said Carol, "I know those mornings."

I was so close to them I could hear the crackle of her cigarette while I guessed she was taking a big breathe-in on it, and then she blew out the smoke.

"It was so quiet," Dad said. "It didn't seem normal the ocean could be that quiet. Minimal waves. Nobody else as far as I could see. I thought about it. I'd get in and wade out farther and farther and farther and just . . . go down. . . ."

I was lying on the counter on my stomach, holding myself up by my elbows, leaning in so close to the window, and then my elbow slid out from under me and I banged my chin right on the faucet.

A blast of pain shot right up my whole jaw. "Uhhh," I said.

They stopped talking.

There was a kind of electric current going in my chest,

and I flopped down from the counter and ran as fast as I could back upstairs, into my room, closed the door, and threw the covers over me. My heart was pounding in my ears and my my chin was throbbing.

What if they'd heard? Maybe they'd think I had just gone down for water or something. I waited a few seconds. No Dad footsteps coming upstairs. Another few seconds. Nothing. I started breathing more normally. I pressed on my chin and it ached.

What did he do after he thought about going down in the water? I didn't want to know but I did want to know. I lay there in bed for a long, long time holding on to Wiley and staring at the shadows on my wall, wondering what Dad and Carol were saying right then.

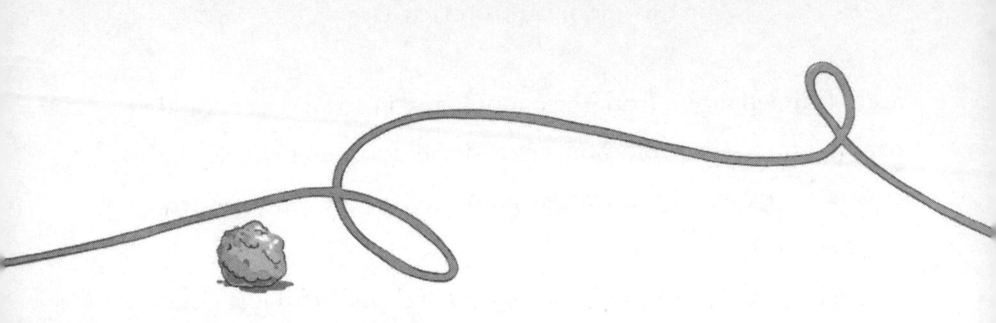

Just Lemon Water

When I got down to the kitchen again that night, I knew I wouldn't eat. Even though I thought I'd heard Dad come up to bed after a while, I peeked out the front window anyway just to check if they might still be there. The porch light was off and there was no one outside.

There were so many dark things weighing on me, and I knew a middle-of-the-night snack wouldn't do anything to help. Still, I had to do something, so I got out a lemon left over from the lemon bars to just squeeze into a glass of water. I couldn't stop thinking about Dad on the beach, about Jean, and about Mom.

If Mom had died in that accident, she wouldn't get to be

on Earth. She wouldn't get to play games and read the newspaper and do those puzzles. Maybe she would be in heaven, or maybe she would be somebody else or a dog. She wouldn't get to play the piano for Helen. She wouldn't get to see me and Nina or eat what we brought her that she used to make us.

But if she had died in that accident, maybe she would remember me from wherever she was. And maybe she could hear me when I talked to her. And I could let her go.

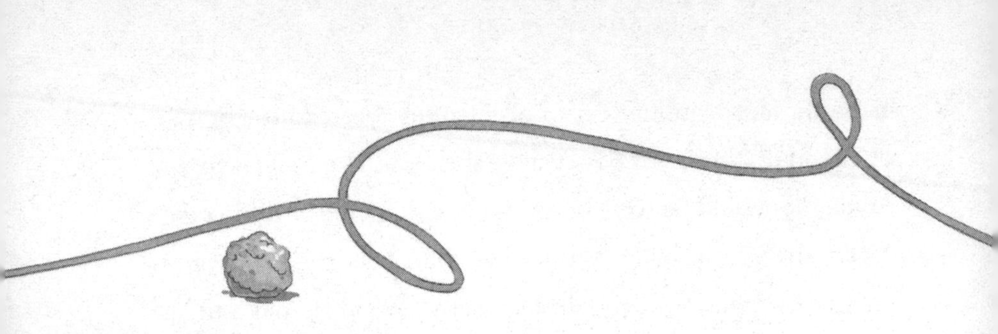

It's Time for Chicken Parmesan

There was something that had to happen. I didn't know what would happen when it happened, but it had to happen. Maybe it was Jean Sawyer's dying that did it. Maybe it gave all of us that feeling of how everything is only for a little while and you kind of have to *do* things that you mean to do "someday" right now, because there may not even be a "someday."

Nina had said something to me about it before I could say it to her. Maybe Dad read our minds a little bit and got nervous or something, because the day after the funeral and family party he came home from work and went right upstairs with a McDonald's bag. The next night we cornered him with chicken Parmesan that he wolfed down just like we thought he would.

Dinner went like this:

Nina said, "Dad, we have to talk to you."

He put down his fork and looked at the table.

"Well," she said, "you should know that Mom asked . . . if you were dead."

My sister, my brave, brave sister was being nice when she said it. Turns out we didn't even have to ask it. Dad smoothed his hair back from his forehead and nodded and said, "It's time, I know." And we knew what he knew. We knew it was time. He was coming home early, he was going to work every day, we hadn't smelled beer breath on him in a while. There were no stashes in the fridge. At all.

It had to be time.

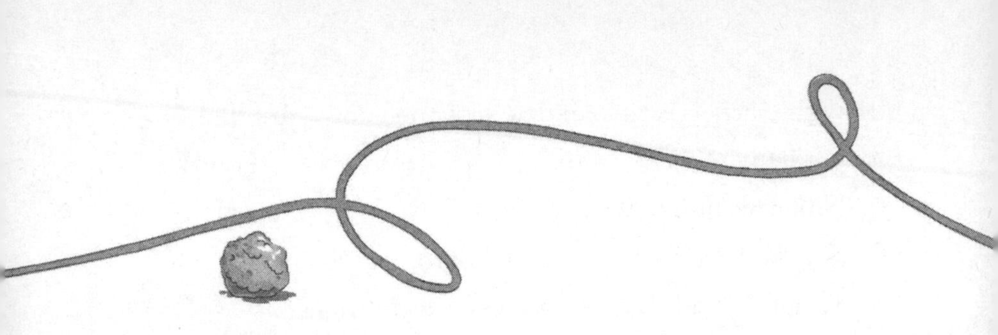

How to Make Cinnamon Rolls

Lisa said sometimes a thing just pulls you toward it. Like her with stars and me with cooking and Nina with dance. Sometimes you gravitate to a thing, Lisa said. Like you almost can't help that you're there doing it—it just had to happen.

Or not happen.

We parked the Honda and we were standing outside the Place and Dad was wiping his hands on his jeans about four thousand times and smoothing his hair back and shifting his weight from one foot to the other. Me and Nina walked past him, and he just stood back for a second.

Then you wouldn't believe it, but he said, "I can't do it.

Not right now. I can't."

"What are you talking about?" asked Nina. "You said you were coming in. You're coming in."

"I know I said it," he said. "But I didn't know . . . I didn't know I would get this feeling . . . ," he said. He sat down, right there on the sidewalk in front the Place. I was looking around to see if anyone was watching.

"I have this pain," he said, holding his chest.

"Just get up, Dad," Nina said. "Oh my God."

Dad sat there on the curb with his head between his knees. He was breathing loudly. It was this mess with us sweating and crying and Nina yelling outside. Helen came out and shooed me and Nina in through the doors. "Girls," she said, "she still needs to see you."

We got ourselves together as we walked down the hall. Mom wore a purple dress, and her hair was curled. She tilted her head to look past us. Their wedding picture was all wrinkled in her hands, and the wedding photo album was next to her on the couch.

"Hi, Mom. It's your girls, Steffy and Nina," said Nina.

"Where's James?" she asked. "I wore the grape jelly dress."

Nina and I looked at each other.

"I don't know where he is, Mom," I said. I hugged her hard and kissed her cheek, and then I had to go into the bathroom because I was holding back a sob.

"You look pretty," Nina was saying in a clear voice as I made my way down the hall.

In the bathroom stall, I pulled way too much toilet paper off the roll, wadded it up, and dabbed my eyes with it. Thank goodness there was no one else in the bathroom right then. I came out and saw myself in the mirror. I thought about how Jean Sawyer had made my mom laugh that day, and in my head I asked her if she could help me somehow do that again today. I wiped my face some more and then went back down hallway D.

"But is he coming?" Mom was saying. Nina looked at me as I sat down.

"Mom," I said, "I love you."

"I love you," she said. I put my arms around her on the couch and took the wedding album out of her hands and she let me, but she kept the one picture of them in her lap.

"Steffy made you cinnamon rolls," said Nina. "The same ones you used to make."

"She said he's coming today," she said, looking toward the lobby. "Helen said."

"Mom," I said, "you and your sister, Gina, used to make these when you had leftover pie-crust dough."

We couldn't get her to eat or play gin rummy or Uno. While we talked about everything but Dad, she stared forward like she wasn't in the same room with us. I kept making the picture in my head of Helen walking him in with her arm around him and then Mom and Dad hugging and then all of us hugging, my family. All the pieces of my family all together and the picture blurred in my brain and it was closer than ever and it made my mouth go dry.

My mom and sister were right there. And my dad was just down hallway D and outside, right in front of the Place. It was like having all the best gnocchi-meal ingredients laid out on the counter: farm fresh eggs, hand-picked potatoes, a loaf of bread still warm from the Harris Teeter, freshly grated Romano cheese. All waiting, all ready. But I wasn't allowed to put it all together.

Mom kept clutching that picture and I kept telling her that you first shape the leftover pie-crust dough into long, thin strips, then you lay them on a cookie sheet, then you sprinkle with cinnamon and sugar, and then you roll them up like snails and bake them. Nina just sat and bit her nails. We got her to try a roll and then she had another and then another.

Nina rubbed Mom's back and said Denise's mom was a hair stylist and manicurist and that she could give her a private appointment. Mom said to ask Helen. Everything ended up sort of okay, but that one wedding picture never did leave her fingers. And not once did Mom laugh or even smile.

After we hugged her good-bye, we headed down hallway D. Outside, Auntie Gina was there, talking to Helen, and the red car was gone.

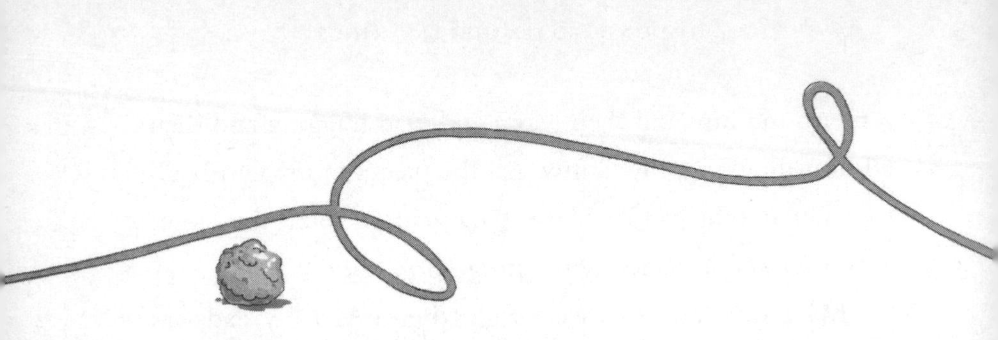

The Cupboard Is Bare

No keys in the dish.
No stash.
Just a damp towel in the bathroom.

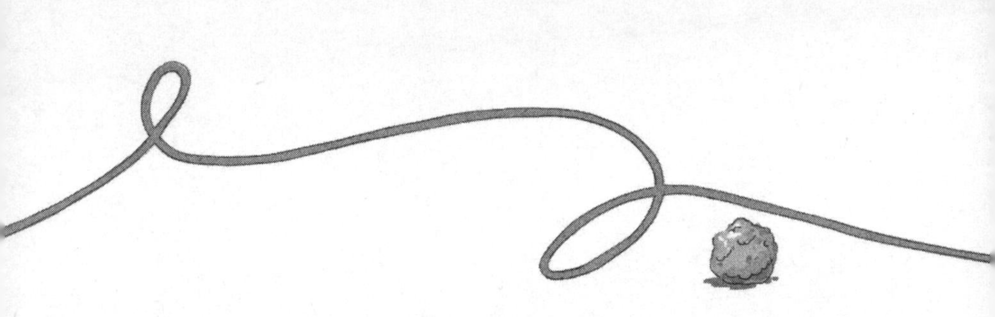

Hungry

No duffel bag.

No shoes.

Just an envelope for me in my room. "Autobiography. From Dad."

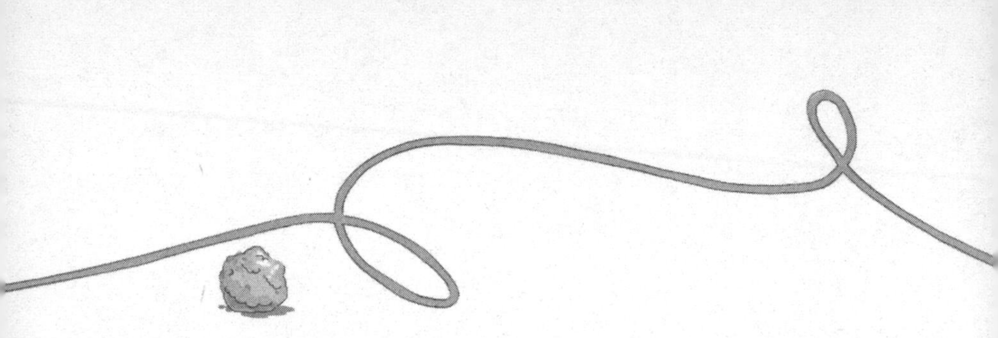

Parsley

Auntie Gina was waiting downstairs for me and Nina to grab some stuff so we could come spend the night with her and Harry. I closed my door, careful not to make the knob click loudly into the lock. I was supposed to be hurrying. But I sat on the floor and unfolded the paper.

Dear Steffany,

I was surprised that you asked me to write you this letter. It's taken me a while to figure out what to say: what I <u>want</u> to say is that you're my daughter and I love you. But I don't think that would be *fair to you. I don't think I've earned it. But you asked me to write you a letter about what I see in you. What I see in you is a person who's kinda like me, kinda quiet but once she gets talking about something that she likes, you can't stop her. And someone who can cook up a mess of Brussels sprouts and egg whites better than her own grandpa could. Someone who helps remind me about the good things in life. I hope that this letter is all right.*

Your dad

I looked up from my dad's letter, and my eyes locked right on the ice cream sundae bank on my dresser. I remembered the five dollars in there that he gave me and Nina on our first day of school. I tossed the letter on the floor and got up and fished out the five dollars. I ripped it. Ripped it and ripped it and ripped it and ripped it into one thousand pieces, until it looked like parsley all over my floor.

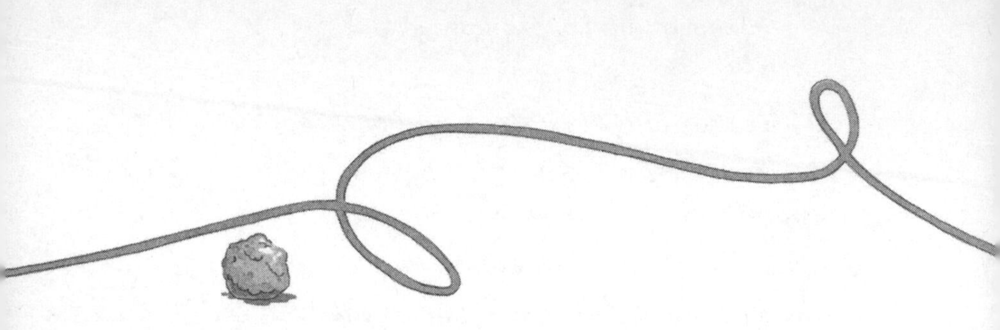

Snacks in Bed

We had rooms at Auntie Gina's, all ready for us for whenever we wanted. It was supposed to be fun spending the night there, like being at a hotel, but all I wanted to do was hide. Tomorrow was Memorial Day, so no school, thank goodness, and then Tuesday the autobiography was due.

I stayed in my "Auntie Gina" room all that Monday off and just lay there. Bare walls and a vacuumy smell. Lots brighter than my room at home because it faced east.

Nina knocked on the door around lunchtime.

"Stef," she said, "eat."

She left waffles on a paper plate at the foot of the bed,

and they just stayed there while I kind of dozed off. Auntie Gina was doing a double shift at the hospital that day, and she kept calling to check in. Harry was also working and would be home later that night. I pretended to be asleep when Nina peeked in to say Gina was on the phone.

Later in the day I started working on the autobiography. Nina kept bringing me snacks. Granola bars and string cheese. Crackers. I just left it all at the foot of the bed with the waffles.

I laid out the four pages of notes of stories Auntie Gina told me and read over what I had for the autobiography so far. Then I sat there for a minute on Auntie Gina's bed. If I was going to be honest, the thing that Mrs. Ashton had been telling us over and over again all year, then I needed to write something else. I tore all the pages that I had clean in half.

All those stories weren't really my stories—they were someone else's memories. I was going to have to start over and write something real. Something that I remembered. And I didn't care about being last-minute. I didn't care about anything. I didn't even care about Chefs of Tomorrow like I used to. Who knew if my dad would come to it anyway?

When the room got a little darker and I had to turn on the lamp, and after Nina had talked on the phone to Auntie Gina again, she came in and made me drink orange juice and it felt good and sweet, and she went down and got me another glass. And then another.

I was kind of starting to get this buzzy headache, and the

next time Nina came in, she had toast on a paper plate that she put on my lap.

"Stef."

"What?"

"Cut it out."

She lifted up the toast to my mouth. I took it from her. I ate the whole thing.

When she was on the phone with Denise in her room, I went and sprawled out on the couch downstairs with my mom's cookbook, recipes spilling on the floor, Harry's laptop nearby, and my English notebook. Starting over meant making a new plan.

Harry got home at about eight o'clock, and a few minutes later his cell phone rang.

"Hello? Oh hi, Helen." He looked at me and shrugged his shoulders. I shot up from the couch. Helen never called Harry. Was something wrong?

"Yeah, she's right here," he said. "Okay."

I took the phone. "Hi, girlie," said Helen. "Everything's fine. Update: your mom and I forgot about the letter. Little too much excitement around here. She wrote it, though, and she wants to give it to you, because she knows it's due tomorrow. What can we do here?"

I got this pulling in my heart. Mom had remembered. When I had forgotten.

Harry ended up getting right back in his car and driving

all the way over to the Place to pick it up for me. I couldn't look at him when he handed me the envelope. "Thanks," I said.

"Welcome, Steffy," he said. He put his hand out and I held it, and we just stood there for a second. The feeling of squeezing a dad-type person's big and sort of rough hand broke something inside of me, and I let go and turned to plop back on the couch. "You almost done?" he asked. "It's getting close to ten."

"I don't know," I said. "But it's due tomorrow, so I have to do it."

Once he was upstairs, I opened the letter.

Hi, Steffany,

When James didn't come, you didn't seem to think it was stupid of me to wear the purple dress for him. You didn't seem to worry that he wasn't there. You brought me cinnamon rolls. That crust was my mother's recipe. You didn't tell me it was okay that James didn't come. You didn't tell me that maybe he'd come another day. You didn't say anything to try and cover up that it was truly awful.

And you made it into that big contest! You are so talented, I know you are.

I want to tell you one more thing and it's this: remember that life could suddenly veer off and leave you stunned and changed forever. You and your sister and my sister are the only rafts I have that keep me afloat. After every one of your visits, I have to go to my room and be alone for a while so I can try to hold on to you for as long as I can and remember all that I am supposed to be. I love you.

Love,
Mom

Cheerios and Toast for Dinner

In the morning, I was so hungry I ate the eggs that Harry had cooked and fruit and two muffins. I even started a third. Auntie Gina gave me her letter for my autobiography as she pulled up to Greensboro Four.

"Now who's Last-Minute Lucy?" I said. She bowed her head and smiled.

"I know," she said. "You're right."

"Thanks," I said.

"Steffy," she said, "I love you, my girl. We'll talk tonight, okay?"

"Okay," I said.

"And I'm stopping at the store this morning before my shift. You need anything?"

"No," I said.

"Practice ingredients?" she asked. I shook my head and got out of the car. It felt weird for me and Nina to be getting to school in Auntie Gina's car and not on our bikes. There wasn't enough time to fill Lisa in on everything, but I told her a little and her jaw dropped when I talked about Dad at the Place. She just stopped, put down her backpack, and hugged me.

The day moved in slow motion, and all I wanted was to be at home, in my own bed. At lunch, Principal Schmitz-Brady came and told me that they were mentioning in the Greensboro Four end-of-the-year newsletter that I was going to be a finalist in Chefs of Tomorrow, and it would say the time and date when people could watch the live broadcast. I pretended that was great but just wanted to go home and go to sleep. The contest was two and a half weeks away. I didn't know if I could get myself to do it. I would rather have had Dad back than have become a finalist. I knew how hard I tried to get my recipes good and all, how many pies I had made, and how many pounds of potatoes I'd boiled for practice gnocchi over the last few months, but it didn't feel like anything right then. All I wanted was for my dad to still be here. For there to still be a chance.

When it finally got to be last period, I took out my autobiography and looked around at other people's. Mine was really, really long compared to most people's. Uh-oh.

I realized I hadn't read Auntie Gina's letter and quickly unfolded it.

Sautéed Steffany Sandolini
by Gina Sandolini

1 cup perseverance
⅔ cup observer
2 pounds talent
1 tablespoon loyalty
dash stubbornness

Pour cup of perseverance over observer and mix together over low heat. Brown talent on both sides over olive oil until it reaches 165 degrees. Add loyalty and stubbornness. Pour sauce over talent and serve with rice and grilled vegetables.

It made me smile but I just wanted to turn it in, and I was so tired my head hurt. Finally bringing up the assignment and putting it on the pile made the pressing on my chest go away a little.

At the end of the day, Nina went to dance with Denise, and I was getting a ride home with Lisa. Right about a block away from St. Theresa's I asked her dad if he could please just stop off there for a minute because they had left a pie pan there for me from a pie I donated a while back. I knew it kind of sounded weird but he said okay, and while Lisa and him waited in the car I ran in.

I wished for my dad. I wished he'd be in the basement, but when I got down there, it was empty of course. The folding chairs were all stacked up on this rolling cart thing in a corner, and the tables were folded and leaning against a wall. There was the faint smell of cigarettes though. I would come back down here again somehow. Maybe I would find Dad.

No one was home at Auntie Gina's when I got dropped off. Lisa said bye and she loved me, and I said bye and I loved her. My instructions were to let myself in and that Auntie Gina and Harry would be home after their shifts, like around nine that night. Nina would be home after dance.

The kitchen was all cluttered with boxes that came in the mail that said Macy's and Crate&Barrel and Williams-Sonoma. Wedding gifts. Also there was a big box with the name of the wedding dress place that we went to together. I guessed Auntie Gina had picked up her dress.

Auntie Gina had bought me yams that were sitting on the counter, and there were tomato sauces and pastes that stared at me when I opened the cabinet for cereal. All these little reminders about Chefs of Tomorrow, but I just wanted to hide from those ingredients that I was once so excited about. I went on the Chefs of Tomorrow website and saw my actual name printed on there, along with the other finalists.

After two bowls of Cheerios and a piece of peanut butter toast, I went up to my room and got into bed, even though it was only five thirty. Never ever would I have cereal for dinner, but I just couldn't bring myself to go into the cabinets and put a meal together. I woke up a while later and it was pitch-dark out, and Auntie Gina and Nina were in my room, on my bed.

Auntie Gina said, "Steffy, I'm sorry to wake you. You have to know that I have been thinking of you and Nina all the last two days and just really had to work. Can you wake up a little so we can talk? You know that everything's going to be okay."

Everything feels very not okay.

"I'm heading to the Harris Teeter again tomorrow," she said. "You need anything special?" Her hand stroked my hair. I was lying with Wiley, facing the wall.

I need to know where my dad is and what is going on.

"You're still doing Chefs of Tomorrow, right?" asked Nina.

Why aren't you talking about my dad, either of you? Why are you talking about stupid things that don't matter?

No one was saying the thing that everyone was thinking. If they weren't going to talk about the most important thing, then I wasn't going to talk about *any*thing.

When they left, and when I was in the place between

awake and asleep, I was imagining Auntie Gina opening that wedding dress box. And then I was imagining Mom before her wedding, before putting on her dress, before holding our dad's hand, before marrying him. How she looked, how she felt, what she thought her life would be.

The Water's Boiling

Nina, with her hair in a bun and wearing her sweats, slid her dance bag over her shoulder while Harry lifted her suitcase out of the trunk. She had her cell phone and earphones in her hands, and she wore a little eyeliner, too, like most of the rest of them. All the girls were laughing and talking, and their excitement just made the rotting feeling in my stomach worse. My sister was leaving again, right when I needed her most. Just like going to Denise's on Christmas.

She even got to have her last day of school be the day before the *real* last day of school so she could ride the bus that Charlotte Rep was sending for the top-scoring girls from Greensboro. It turned out that she wouldn't have needed Dad to drive her down after all.

Nina always got everything she wanted. When it was my turn to hug her, she went with her arms around my waist and squeezed, and I was limp. It went like this:

"Steffy, just think, tomorrow's the last day of school, and soon it's Chefs of Tomorrow. Everything's gonna be fine."

Now something in me was simmering, and I didn't know if I could keep the lid on. She kept saying how fine everything was. Just fine. It'll all be fine, don't worry.

"It's *not* fine, because whenever anything's wrong, you leave," I said.

"That's not fair."

"Yeah, it's not fair that you can just leave whenever you want. You always do whatever you want and don't think about anyone else." The words were coming out of me fast.

"Shut up, Steffany. I would never tell you not to go and do your thing. You know what? Get your stubborn little passive-aggressive butt into the freakin' kitchen to practice for the finals next Sunday. You're not doing the one thing you love doing, and that's what's making you act like this. It's not Dad, it's not Mom, it's *you*."

The simmer in me turned into a rolling boil. Denise and her mom were sort of looking at us. Miss Ronnie was herding girls up onto the bus. When Nina turned to go get on the bus, I launched forward like a rocket, and I punched her in the back. She turned around real fast, our noses almost touching.

"Grow up," she said.

"You grow up!"

Then Harry was pulling my arm, and people were trying to look away but weren't. Miss Ronnie's face was pointed somewhere else, but her eyes were on us.

When we were headed back to Auntie Gina and Harry's, Harry said, "Good for you, Steffany." Auntie Gina kind of slugged him.

She knocked on my door later that night.

"You want pie?" she asked.

"No. I want to talk now."

"Okay."

"Auntie Gina, what's going to happen when you get married and Dad doesn't come back? I don't know what to do or how I'm supposed to . . . supposed to be!"

She sat and rocked me for a long, long time. Waves of feeling kept coming up and coming up, and Auntie Gina went out twice for tissues.

"I'm sorry," I said.

"For what?"

"Sometimes I wish . . . I wish you weren't so nice to take in me and Nina. I didn't want you to be. I wanted them. I wanted . . . my dad to . . . not leave."

"Well," said Auntie Gina after a second, "can I tell you a secret, and promise not to get mad at me?"

I turned my face to see her eyes. I nodded. "Promise?" she asked again. I nodded.

"Well. I was never trying to be nice by taking you and

Nina. I just couldn't see any other option than you guys being with me. When your mom's accident happened, I knew you like she knew you. Saw you every day, changed your diapers and fed you, had sleepovers with you. Your dad and I even said that maybe I should move in with you guys, just to be there for you and Nina. And then, Steffy, I got home from the hospital, from seeing your mom right after the accident, and he was just gone. Like, disappeared. And there were you and Nina. And I knew you guys. I knew that you loved all foods and would play with anything, and that Nina only ate three or four things and only wanted to play with trucks or dress-up. I knew when you napped, and I knew how to calm Nina down from a tantrum."

It was like a waterfall of all of the stuff from my life, and I wanted her to keep telling me and telling me.

"And now that everything is said and done, and your dad is gone again, my secret is," she said, bending down and whispering in my ear, "as much as you wanted your dad to be with you . . . I wanted you to be with me."

I tucked my head in, right into her shoulder, and we just sat there for a long time.

I remembered when I was really little and got scared at night I'd sneak down the shadowy hallway and into the back bedroom, and Auntie Gina'd say, "Well, you can either stay in bed with me for a little bit and then walk back to your room all by yourself, or I can carry you back in right now." I always chose the carrying back.

Roasting Marshmallows

Mrs. Ashton passed back our autobiography projects on the last day of school. It was an early-dismissal day and then there was this good-bye-lunch thing that you could go to if you wanted. I'd said good-bye to everyone I'd miss, and I was sleeping over at Lisa's that night anyway. Instead of staying for the lunch, we walked to St. Theresa's, which was probably too far for us to walk but we knew exactly where we were going and we were officially sixth graders now. It was so easy to just go in and sneak right down to the basement.

"Oh my gosh," she whispered when I told her about the meetings. "Right here?" she asked. "You just sit right here and they don't see you?"

I pointed to my step—the third step from the top—and

showed her how I hugged my knees and leaned against the wall and craned my head down a little bit for a perfect view.

"Mission accomplished, Steffany. Oh my gosh."

"I need to come back tomorrow somehow," I said.

"You can," she said. "We'll ride over. I still have my old bike."

"All the way from your house?"

"Steffy, it's not that far."

"It's farther than mine is," I said.

"So?"

"But I don't even know if he'll be here for sure," I said.

"But he might," she said. "I have a feeling about it. And my feelings are usually right."

The next morning we said we were going to take a bike ride, and Lisa's mom said that sounded good. She made us promise to be back in an hour and we said we would. And she made us both wear helmets and knee pads and Lisa rolled her eyes, and as I Velcro-ed everything on, I thought about the basement and hoped Lisa wasn't doing all this for me for nothing.

She was right. It really wasn't that far. And her old bike was just like my bike, and it felt so good to get back on it and let it carry me. It took about fifteen minutes to get there, but it was uphill.

"Coming back's gonna be quicker," she said. "Come on."

We parked and locked up our bikes out front. There was

no mass this early on Saturdays, and there were just the usual old ladies in a few pews here and there. Lisa sat in the last pew with her book, and there was this big, swelling feeling in me and I couldn't swallow for a second as I watched her just sit there, waiting for me. My very best friend in the world.

I made sure we got there just a little bit after I thought the meeting started so I wouldn't risk someone seeing me go down. But there was another door that I thought they came in through anyway, down a slope in the back of the church that was an entrance right into the basement.

I tiptoed downstairs.

Dad.

Standing up front.

I almost called out to him.

Oh my gosh, my plan worked. It worked, it worked, it worked. There was a zippy, jittery feeling coursing through me, and I held my breath and hugged my knees tight.

He stood with his hands folded, one foot crossed in front of the other, looking at the cement floor for a minute.

"But that morning," he was saying, "it made so much sense to me for some reason. It would be easy. And I . . . I mean, I had nothing. I'd gotten evicted again. I had no job."

He stopped to take a long sip of his Styrofoam cup drink.

"And I . . . I don't know if anyone's ever tried it, or thought about it."

People nodded their heads.

"I just, I . . . went in. To the water."

These words came out slow.

"I got as far as my neck."

No one was drinking their drinks. No one was moving or even breathing, maybe.

"And then something really simple happened," Dad said. "The sun just started rising. And I watched the whole thing. That big, giant ball of fire that keeps us alive. And I stood there. And I realized that—because I could feel the sun now—I hadn't felt how ice cold the water was. And I thought, if there's one thing—one thing I need to do in my life before I die, it's go back to my daughters. Go back to my wife."

Dad stood there, nodding slowly. He took a sip of his drink.

It was that same you're-gonna-get-in-trouble feeling, knowing these things. Me and Nina and Mom were what had made my dad come out of the water.

"But that time—in the water?" he said. "That's not even the half of it. Not even close."

I was getting a hot feeling in my chest, and I just knew I couldn't hear any more. There was a rushing feeling, like something was beating me up the stairs so quick I didn't even have time to decide to go.

It was like when you're roasting a marshmallow, and it accidentally catches fire. You yank it out real quick, without even thinking about it. But then you have this on-fire marsh-mallow, and so you blow it out. Once it's done burning, you see that it's black.

And I felt black right then. I couldn't believe it, but I wanted to not know everything now. I wished I hadn't gone down. I wished I hadn't made Lisa come here with me. I wished me and Nina hadn't ever made our dad try to go see Mom.

I just wanted to be back at our house, with my dad, making him eggs with lots of pepper. I just wanted the coffeemaker on and I wanted the sound of the newspaper wrinkling between his fingers.

Getting Excited Again about Being a Chef

Her phone rang once and then she picked up.

"Hey, Steffy, just a sec," Nina said. Then she finished saying something about a pair of sweatpants and then people started laughing and she said, "I told you it was ridiculous." And then she said, "Hi, what's up?" into the phone.

"Nina . . . ," I said.

She paused. "Can I meet you guys down there?" she said to the other voices in the room with her. "It's my sister."

I told her about my plan with Lisa.

I told her about Dad.

I told her what he said.

"Oh my God," she said.

We just sat there on the phone with each other, not saying anything. Which felt really, really good.

"Oh my God," she said again.

"I know," I said.

"Well," she said, "he didn't do it. That's good. I guess."

"What do mean, you guess?" I asked.

"I don't know, Steffy."

We sat on the phone some more.

"No," she said, "I mean, of course it's good he didn't do it."

We didn't know what to say next. But just hearing Nina breathe from Charlotte was probably the only thing that could have made me feel better.

"Steffy," she said, "there's nothing really to do about it. I mean . . . it's like, sad, and everything, but what are we gonna do? Just get ready for Chefs of Tomorrow and do really well and just . . . pretend like Dad never came."

"But he did come."

"Yeah, and now he's gone."

"Yeah," I said. "But he's not *gone*. He was there. I saw him."

"True," she said. "But . . . that doesn't mean he's coming back. And honestly, I don't know if I want him to. Ever again."

We got nothing solved about Dad, but I'd never needed to hear Nina's voice more than right then.

"Steffy, this is supposed to be a surprise, but guess who's

waking up at the crack of dawn next Saturday, getting on an early bus, and coming up to G-boro for her sister's cooking competition?"

It was a whole combination of things that made me get excited about Chefs of Tomorrow again: the smell of the mashed potatoes that I had made the day before, talking to Nina that night after hearing Dad's story and hearing that she was coming to surprise me, maybe getting a good night's sleep. And there I was, an official finalist, ready to cook.

They put up these giant platforms, right on the baseball field, and made kitchens on each of them. The five of us were each set up with our ingredients. Just like an actual TV cooking show.

Bob Sebuda himself came over and told us all about the big digital clock beside the screen to the left of the audience. He said that a camera would come near us while we cooked and not to be nervous. Men and ladies in jeans and T-shirts pushed around cameras. Giant spotlights shone on each platform, even though it was daytime.

Auntie Gina and Harry and Nina were waving from the front row with Mrs. Ashton. Lisa and her mom and dad were sitting off to the side near the front. I couldn't help imagining Dad appearing in the crowd somewhere, but there was too much else happening to think about it for long.

Someone came out with a big sign that said Applause and

talked to the audience about clapping loudly. A lady dashed over to Bob Sebuda and dabbed his forehead with a makeup sponge, and then all of a sudden, music started.

"This is Bob Sebuda live from Grasshopper Stadium at New Bridge Bank Park," said Bob. And the crowd cheered. A guy filming them got pushed along the front row on a cart.

"We have transformed the Hoppers' stomping grounds into a gourmet's paradise," he said, "and we now bring you the five finalists from our nine-to-twelve category, in the first annual Chefs of Tomorrow contest." He then congratulated the kids who had already won in the family category, and he reminded the audience that the finalists from the thirteen-to-seventeen category would compete that evening. More clapping from the audience.

He went on to talk about each of us in the nine-to-twelve category, and I was glad Auntie Gina had made me eat a banana before we came because I got dizzy hearing my name that loud, spoken to that many people. I was wiping and wiping my hands on my apron.

There were screens that were showing what was being filmed while it was being filmed, and one was showing me and I was wiping and smiling. I hadn't even realized I was smiling.

"Chefs, time on the clock is one hour and thirty minutes, start to finish. All your ingredients have been preset for you. Are you ready?"

All of us looked at each other from our different little kitchens. The turkey-dinner girl from last time gave a thumbs-up, and people laughed. I nodded, and there was a hot feeling spreading all over my face and chest.

"All right," said Bob, "gentlemen and ladies, you may begin!"

Finally. And you could just feel all of us getting to business. For me, sauce was first. I cut up my sausage and onions and garlic superfast, just like I practiced. Then I fried all this up in olive oil and added the tomato sauce and paste, and before I knew it, the sauce was simmering, and I was on to my dough. There was music playing, and Bob kept talking about I don't know what. My hands were shaking because of the cameras following me every second.

When I had to knead, I gripped and clawed at that dough, and there was the panic that comes with dough, that it's always gonna be a mess. Nina was yelling, "Hoards derves, hoards derves, hoards derves," and it made me laugh and I glanced at myself smiling at the dough on TV, which made me smile bigger and just laugh a little that I was doing this. That I was standing on this giant platform in a fake kitchen *making gnocchi*. I couldn't hear what Bob was saying, but I heard "Sandolini" in there somewhere. The dough was making me too, too nervous because it was all sticky and clumpy, and there were tears ready to come down. But right away I remembered the water secret, and after a few drops, it started becoming whole.

Okay. Dough was cleeshing. One hour and nine minutes left. On to the pie. Preheat oven: check. The yams weren't as soft as I would have liked, but oh well. Once the pie was in the oven, right exactly at fifty minutes left (just as planned!), I went on to the gnocchi slicing and schweeting. No problems there.

I popped some garlic bread in the oven to broil for five minutes. Oh no! I had forgotten to turn on the stove to boil the gnocchi! I ran to the stove and turned it on full blast, clamped the lid over the big pot of water, and looked out for Auntie Gina. She pointed to her watch and nodded.

A camera went close up on my face, and I turned right around like I was real busy and pulled the pie out of the oven, sprinkled the crumble on top, and slid it back in. Dessert: almost done. I set the colander in the sink: ready. I set the table with big plates and pie plates and then with an oven mitt lifted out the garlic bread. Second thought, I put it back in and turned the upper oven off. Better to serve it hot. Time: twelve minutes.

I checked my water, and it was as still as a painting. I filled two glasses with ice and water. Fluffed the flowers in the vase. Tried not to dwell on the stir-fry girl just sitting and fanning herself with a napkin, and the stew kid laughing and nodding at the camera, displaying his meal. They were done ten minutes early!

Checked my water, and there were little bubbles on the sides. Auntie Gina's eyes said just keep going, and I did. I pushed from my brain the cameras all by me now, Bob saying each thing I did as I was doing it. Finally, I got a boil, at six minutes. It'd take me about three minutes to strain and rinse in hot water and then douse with sauce. I dumped in only half of the gnocchi that I'd cut so it'd take quicker. Five minutes left.

Grabbed the garlic bread out of the oven. Four minutes. Stirred the gnocchi. Some were actually beginning to rise to the top. Yes! Three minutes. Slid the pie out of the oven and set it on the table. The audience was clapping and cheering. I risked *one more* gnocchi-boiling minute. But at one minute on the clock I had to turn off the heat, lift the pot, pour the gnocchi into the colander, and rinse. Load up each plate, douse with sauce. Time.

I stepped back from the counter like Bob had said to. I looked around at all my fellow cooks, and everybody was smiling so big. We all looked red and blotchy and relieved. Oh darn, I had forgotten to set out the Romano cheese! Oh well. And there was sauce slopped all over the floor. Eh. I was sure that the other people's kitchens were all messy too, so I just let Bob lead me and the others down to the front, and when they asked me what I was thinking when I realized I'd forgot to turn on the stove to boil the water, all I said was that I thought, "Oh my gosh, I forgot to turn on the stove."

We were allowed to go and sit with our families while the judging happened. Lisa made her way across the front row to grab me and said she could never have finished the way I did. Nina and Auntie Gina were talking nonstop about what everyone did, like the stew boy spilling all his stock and having to use water that he seasoned up with salt and garlic powder, and how the catfish boy burned one of the catfish and only was able to serve one plate of food at the end instead of two, but at the last minute he cut the fish in half and put a piece on each plate.

I looked behind us and into the crowd of people all around, standing and sitting and chatting and laughing a lot. I hoped I would see a tall, blondish guy looking for me. I scanned the audience in every direction. Maybe he was there somewhere and just couldn't find us.

Luckily, the judging was quick, so I didn't have a whole lot of time to think about it. Bob said that this time was even harder than the first time around. He reminded us that the winner got three thousand dollars and to have their meal featured on the menu at Lucky 32. Also, second place was one thousand dollars and summer cooking lessons at Elon University. Third, fourth, and fifth got two hundred and fifty dollars each.

"I don't think I'm going to win," I said.

"Shut up, Steffy," said Lisa.

"You're winning *something*," said Nina. "All five of you

are—you made it this far."

Bob said, "In fifth place: barbecued catfish and king cake!"

The crowd roared.

"Fourth place: Asian noodle stir-fry and vanilla soy cookies!"

Whooping and clapping.

"Third: caramel beef stew with vegetables and caramel apples!"

Screaming and hollering.

Each of the cooks was coming up and shaking hands with Bob and getting an envelope.

Oh my gosh, I either won first or second, I either won first or second, I either won first or second. Everyone in my family was looking at me, but I just stared at Bob and there were flames in my cheeks.

Then he said, "Second place: potato gnocchi and yam-pecan pie!"

And I think I walked up but it was more like I floated up, and everybody was cheering and I shook hands and the stew boy hugged me, and Bob gave me a big envelope and the lights blinded me a little and I squint-smiled toward my family.

The traditional-turkey-dinner girl came up and jumped up and down and got her stuff. There were splatters and splashes all over her apron, and her face was all splotchy, too. Then we all stood together and held hands, and cameras flashed and Bob told us to bow and said we were remarkable. I let myself feel it from underneath my feet to a hovering part over my head.

Harry said that in life there were these rare, monumental things that happen, and he called them Key Moments. He said that when I was up there on that stage, that was a Key Moment. I didn't know if I would ever feel like that again. I didn't know if I could ever do anything as good. I didn't know what I did to deserve it. I just held my envelope and closed my eyes as they filled up behind my lids.

Tummy Ticklers for Little Tots

Auntie Gina once told me about something called neuroplasticity. How some people think that the well part of the brain is always trying to spark the sick part of the brain and get it back on track. She said that in some patients the well part even won, and the sick part got better. Her whole thing about saying only good things around Mom was to help the sick part of her brain get sparked.

That's why me and Auntie Gina brought the whole cookbook with us this time. Since it was summer, we could go visit Mom whenever we wanted, really, and so we changed it to Mondays, when Auntie Gina was off now.

Helen said it was okay to bake, that we could use the

kitchen in the dining hall again. Mom was doing so well lately, reading and remembering, playing music, asking questions. We thought it could be good to cook together again.

After all the big hugs, we gave her her old cookbook. At first she just held it in her lap and then she was almost crying. With her index finger she went back and forth over the red-and-white plaid cover.

"We're making banana bread, Mom," I said. "Will you get the recipe out?" She opened the book slowly and sifted through scrap after scrap and notebook sheet after notebook sheet. I wondered what she thought about reading her old recipes, if looking at them jogged something in her. When she found the banana bread one, she read it out loud to Auntie Gina, who followed the directions. I liked seeing them going back and forth, Auntie Gina talking about how she remembered their mom making up recipes all the time.

"Our mom had a knack," said Mom.

"So do you," said Auntie Gina.

Mom asked, "When did she die?"

"Your senior year of high school," said Auntie Gina. "Steffy, you come stir." I did, and then Mom added the chocolate chips, and then I folded them in. After we got it into the oven, we sat around one of the big dining tables, and Auntie Gina told Mom how I got second place. Mom hugged and hugged me. We also told her that Nina missed her so much and loved it in Charlotte.

Soon the warm chocolate-banana smell filled the kitchen, and the other residents started coming in and asking questions. Helen said it was a treat and anyone was welcome to enjoy some in a bit. All the while Mom studied her old banana bread recipe, her thumbs tight on the sides of the yellowed paper.

"This was from the Mini Page," she said.

"The Mini Page . . . from the *Greensboro Daily News*?" asked Auntie Gina.

"That's where I found this. In the Mini Page—in that section called Tummy Ticklers for Little Tots. I was in fifth grade. Like Steffy."

We were just quiet for a second. Mom's eyes came to life, like maybe the place behind them got a little charge of electricity.

Hi, James Falcon, I'm Gonna Be Doing Cooking Lessons.

"Hey. This is James Falcon. Please leave me your important message after the tone."

My important message was short and easy, and my voice didn't even shake. I just said, "Hi, I came in second and I opened a bank account with the thousand dollars, and I'm gonna be doing cooking lessons. Did you see me on TV? Bye."

I had to at least try to reach him.

The way that I was trying to reach my mom.

Maybe I still didn't know what would happen with my parents in the long run, but my dad and mom could be reached. I could even hug them, touch them.

I wished I could leave Jean Sawyer a message on her voice mail to tell her thank you for letting us live with her when we were little and giving us rides now that we were older, and thank you for taking care of us.

Cake, Cake, Cake, Cake, Cake, and Cake. And Candy. And Cookies.

The wedding cake was the hardest thing I ever made. Harder than Kitchen Sink, harder than Crock-Pot Thanksgiving dinner, harder than gnocchi and pie in an hour and a half. One hundred pieces of cake is a lot of pieces of cake. And what if someone wanted two? And they had to freeze some for luck, said the magazines.

Plus, I knew I was being all ambitious, but I was making a special thing for Harry, too, that I hoped would turn out. This Korean sesame candy that I read about online. And then there were the S's and O's that were in the cookbook in my grandma Sandolini's writing. But I had planned ahead and made those last night and then brought them over to my house to frost them.

We decided that since all Harry's relatives were in town and staying at Harry and Auntie Gina's, we shouldn't do the cake over there. They were here all the way from Korea, and Auntie Gina was worried about his great-aunt Lucy and his grandmother, and she wanted things to be quiet and calm for them.

She had dropped me and all the ingredients off, and she'd be back in a while, as soon as she stopped at the flower place and then St. Theresa's. Harry was getting his tuxedo and then picking up some more cousins from the airport. Nina was on the bus home, and we'd get her this evening before the rehearsal thing.

I thought it'd be weird going back home, but there was too much to do right then besides getting sad and pulled down about my dad. I didn't know what was going to happen next, but me and Nina were fine at Auntie Gina's for now. Any panic I had about what would happen after she was officially married to Harry was way down at the bottom of me somewhere, and at the top was all the flour and sugar and cocoa and vanilla extract and eggs and powdered sugar that was bulging out of the Harris Teeter bags.

Since this was supposed to be a serious cake, I actually made it all from scratch. Mom's cookbook got all splattered with batter and vanilla and cooking oil. The kitchen was exploding with measuring cups, small mixing bowls, big mixing bowls. The spatula, dishcloths, a pile of sugar that

I spilled on the counter, mixing spoons, eggshells. Basically everything from the cabinets was out.

I had made six cakes because I imagined mad people who wanted a second piece and decided it was better to have more cake (what better thing to have more of than less of?) than not enough. I think I had the oven on for about five hours total and the air-conditioning cranked up high. I sang to the radio full blast.

I didn't hear the screen door creaking open. I didn't hear the keys. I didn't hear Dad until he was right there saying, "Hey."

I said, "Dad!" And then I rushed to turn the music down.

His muscly arms dangled by his sides.

"Smells great," he said.

"Yeah. Wedding cake," I said, wiping my forehead. "And cookies. And this sesame candy thing."

Dad handed me a box, and inside was an apron. A really cool orange apron with my name on it. Spelled right, which means he must have had it made at a special place. On the counter, he put a little bag with a card that said "Nina" and a card that said "Gina and Harry."

"They here?" he asked.

I shook my head.

"Nina go to Charlotte?" he asked.

I nodded. He nodded. He wiped his hands on his jeans, and I put on the apron.

"Steffany," he said. "Got your message. I am proud to be your dad. And Nina's. I'm not . . . proud of much right now. But that's one thing."

I just held my elbows and watched him walk toward the door. He dropped the keys in the dish and put his hand on the knob. He was just gonna go. Just walk out.

"Where are you going?" I asked.

He froze there with his hand on the doorknob. The oven started to beep. As I turned off the heat and pulled oven mitts over my hands, I got more guts. If I could go on TV and cook a meal, I could talk to my own dad. I slid the cake pans out of the oven, put them on the counter, and faced him again.

"And why? *Why* are you going?" I asked. "Is it because of something that we did? Are you mad at us?"

"No," said Dad. He let go of the doorknob. "I'm not mad at you. Put that out of your mind and never think it again. It's complicated, Steffy."

"I do complicated math at school. I'm in the A group."

He rubbed the stubble on his cheeks and chin.

"I need to go and work some things out," he said.

"You could *stay* and work some things out," I said.

"I don't think I can right now," he said. "Everything . . ."

That word just hung there along with the smell of vanilla cake.

"Everything will be okay," he said.

"No," I said. I took off the oven mitts and threw them

on the table. "Everyone always says that." I walked right up to Dad. "I was very mad at you."

He stood up straight and pulled his head back a little.

"Mom wanted to see you. She was all ready to see you. Why did you do that?"

He turned around in the doorway. "I'm sorry, Steffany," he said. "I have to go now. *I really have to go now.*" The words sounded like they had weights tied to them.

"Wait one second," I said. "Please."

I ran over to the sink. I didn't know I needed to do this until it happened: I lifted the old picture of Mom off the wall—the mom who looked like the person she was when she got married—and I ran back to Dad with my arm stretched out. He took the picture.

I blurted out what I'd wanted to say since I'd read his letter: "You could say you love me."

He put his head down on his chest, and his shoulders hunched forward. It was like he deflated. He whispered, "I don't know who I am, Steffany. I'm sorry." He backed up, holding the picture of Mom, and was out the door.

His keys stayed in the dish.

The Biggest Cleesh

"Auntie Gina," I said, "it's your Key Moment." And she was instantly crying, and we hugged. Her dress with the purple sash matched up perfectly with the purple crepe myrtle that Harry wore pinned to his lapel, and the spaghetti-strap dresses me and Nina wore, too. I'd never been to a wedding, let alone been *in* one. Nina either. Thank goodness our dresses had these secret bra things built in, and the elastic part on the chest wasn't itchy at all. Denise's mom had come and done up our hair. It felt like there was a wedding cake on my head.

Mom looked beautiful, all in purple and silver, her hair down. Helen sat with her in the back, near the vestibule in case they had to go to the bathroom. I liked seeing her out of the Place and in the world.

Once the service in the church was over, we took pictures on the lawn while the guests ate pigs in a blanket and drank Cheerwine. Then the reception started right out back, and the meal was laid out on this long table. At one end were the plates and glasses and silverware. Spread along the middle of the table was the feast: ziti and salad, garlic bread, meatballs, rice and vegetables, kimchi, and these garlicky pancake things called *pa jun* that I have to learn to make. It all looked perfect.

And there, and at the other end of the table, were all the desserts: the layer cake, the cookies, and the sesame candy. It all really turned out. Even the cake layers actually looked good, like they weren't too lopsided or amateurish. Each layer was a different flavor, from carrot at the top, and then it alternated: vanilla, chocolate, vanilla, chocolate, vanilla.

For the dinner, I got to sit in between Mom and Helen, and Nina sat across from us. Mom's eyes were all watering the whole time, but she said how much she loved being out. It was warm, and the flowers in Helen's hair shimmied with the breeze. Me and Nina couldn't stop giggling at everything.

I am not being all conceited when I say that everyone loved the desserts. I mean, after you eat all that main course stuff, you're going to want dessert, so there you go. Harry came over to me special, his eyes watering, with a piece of sesame candy in his hand and picked me up in a big hug.

Afterward, when everyone started dancing, I went and ladled up another cup of sweet tea. I thought about Mom and Dad being so young when they did this, how maybe they weren't even cleeshed yet on their own, so how could they be ready to cleesh together? But Auntie Gina and Harry were. They just *were*.

When I had my tea, I went and sat with Harry's great-aunt Lucy, who said, "Hello, Miss Gourmet. I heard it's congratulations for you." I thanked her very much. She said she used to own a restaurant in Korea and that my sesame candy was the perfect nuttiness. I didn't feel silly talking about wanting people to like what I made. Aunt Lucy nodded and took my palm in her hands, and there was something that she pressed into my hand. A dollar.

"Your first customer. Frame it in your restaurant." I couldn't stop smiling.

Later on, watching Mom and Nina dancing, I kind of was figuring out the thing about why you needed to be remembered. Being remembered was when someone ate what you made for them. It was an exchange. If you cooked and it just sat there, well, 1) it would get cold, 2) it would be a waste of ingredients, and 3) you needed to share it to have it all mean something. Being remembered was me expressing myself, like Auntie Gina told me to, and it being *accepted*. And devoured.

Nina walked Mom over to Helen, who gave Mom some water, and then my sister went and danced with Harry's dad and everyone laughed. And there was a cousin of Harry's who was sixteen, and she danced with him, too, even some of the slow dances.

I just watched everyone. All Harry's family, all Korean, shaking around and looking kind of silly on the dance floor with all the Italian Sandolinis who were looking equally silly (except for Nina, the dancer). All of us there for one thing—one big party for Auntie Gina and Harry—and it came to me that bringing two families together was the biggest cleesh you could ever do.

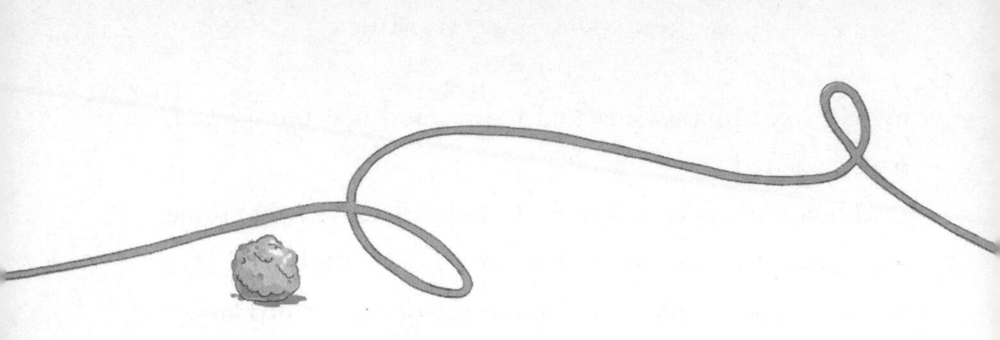

Hands to Heart to Handwriting

Kneading the dough a few days after the wedding got me all funny, and I was imagining Mom's hands doing it. After all the times making gnocchi this year, it was in my palms and my fingers and knuckles. I knew pasta by heart because I'd watched Auntie Gina make it so many times and then I tried it and tried it and tried it some more. I guessed Mom and Auntie Gina had learned the same way—nobody ever wrote it all down.

I thought of the banana bread recipe and how I felt when I read down that list. How Mom might have felt when she was my age and she wrote it out. What she might have been thinking about. How she wanted everything to go.

The part of Mom's letter about life veering off had been haunting me. So later, while the dough was setting, I did something. I got out construction paper and markers that I used when I sometimes made place cards for big family dinners, and I wrote out the whole gnocchi recipe in my best handwriting. I included all the steps, from cutting up onions and garlic for the sauce to tasting testers after the pasta's boiled for a little while. I wrote each step down in my best handwriting for someone to maybe read later, in case they couldn't watch me make it.

Birthday Cupcakes

It was the day before Mom's birthday—the last of Harry's relatives had gone, and the blankets me and Nina had slept with on the couch were folded and stacked back in the closet. Before I could even notice how desperately I needed to know what was going to happen to me and Nina now that all the excitement was done, now that Dad had left, Auntie Gina sat us all down.

"Girls," she said. "Okay." She looked up, and her eyes started to water. "So much to say," she said, "now that I can actually say it. And I need to get this out before we take Nina back to Charlotte in a couple days."

Harry took her hand. She cleared her throat.

"I thought, when you went to live with your dad . . . I thought that it would be really hard for you," she said, putting her hand on her mouth and then taking it off, "because you were going to need me so much. And that made me feel bad. And guilty." She swallowed. "But what I found out was . . . how grown-up and well-adjusted and strong you girls are, and I found out that instead of you needing me so much, I was needing you. . . ."

And then we were all needing tissues.

"Gina and I are wondering," said Harry, "what you guys would think about living here with us. For good. For keeps."

I looked at Nina, and she turned to me.

"We don't even want you to say anything right now," Harry said. "We just want you to think about it."

"I already know my answer," said Nina. "But you got to say your thing. Now I get to say mine." She stood up. Crossed her arms. "I don't hate Dad," she said. "But if ever again we suddenly have to live with him, that will be so not fair. And I will so not do it."

She turned around. "Sorry," she said as she walked through the kitchen and down the hallway. "I'm not trying to be rude."

Auntie Gina was just nodding and wiping her nose.

"I think I know my answer, too," I said. "But I have to think about it."

That night I fell right asleep. When I came down at about

eleven the next morning, Auntie Gina was halfway through schweeting gnocchi, and Nina was frosting cupcakes. I got to helping, and while we worked, no one talked about what Auntie Gina and Harry had said last night. A little bit later, when things were all put in containers and dishes were in the dishwasher, Auntie Gina pulled us both into her, and the three of us stood there, holding on to each other.

"Thank you," said Nina, and right then and there, we knew both our answers to Auntie Gina's question.

We brought everything to Mom's that afternoon. Helen had hats for all of us, and the other residents came around to sing when Mom blew out the candles. Harry came, too, and even though she had to be reminded of who he was, she let him hug her and kiss her.

Later, Auntie Gina said she had something important to talk to Mom about, and she sat down real close to her on the couch. Helen came and sat on Mom's other side.

"Okay," said Helen, "but we have something important to talk to you about, too."

Auntie Gina's eyes got bright when she heard that, but she asked if she could go first. "I just need to get this out into the open," she said. Helen winked at Auntie Gina. Me and Nina sat on the other couch, holding hands. Harry stood behind us.

Auntie Gina turned to Mom. "I love you," she said, "and

I love the girls. I have thought and thought and thought." She wiped her eyes. "I wanted to ask you if it would be okay with you if Harry and I put in paperwork to adopt. The girls. They would make us so happy."

Nina squeezed my hand hard. Auntie Gina and Helen and Mom and Harry talked some more.

It was officially out in the open.

If our mom said it was okay, we would officially move into the cozy house with the soda-making machine and the backyard and the millions of bedrooms and closets. Auntie Gina and Harry had postponed their honeymoon to Italy so we could get settled in. It didn't feel real yet, though. I didn't quite know how I felt about the whole thing. It was another Giant New Thing this year, and I was so, so tired of that.

But then there was something else.

"James came," Mom said while she was blotting her eyes with a tissue. "James came to see me."

"He came?" I asked. "My dad was here?" I asked Helen. She nodded slowly, a smile creeping onto her face. Auntie Gina had a look on her face like she was half mad, half glad. "Oh my God," she said. "He finally did it."

I leaped off the couch. "Mom," I said. "He came! That's good!" And I turned back to Auntie Gina and Harry, and there was a catch in my heart. I put my hand on my neck like a real fishhook caught me by the throat. If Dad had come here and if Mom got better someday, maybe we could really be a family, our *real* family. Mom stood up and turned me around to face her. She looked at Helen as she spoke.

"Your dad wants you to live with Gina."

"You guys talked about it?" I asked.

"We did," Mom said. I looked at Helen, who nodded.

"But we're . . . being given away," I said.

"Oh no," said Mom. "No, no, no, no," she said, and I buried my face in her shoulder.

All the times we had visited, all the Sundays of my whole life, it was us making Mom feel better. It was us telling her all the good things she was doing and how she was getting better. And now it was her helping me to feel better.

"I don't ever want to hear you say that," she whispered in my ear. "When Helen says I can move out of here," she said, "I'm coming to live with you, too." I glanced at Helen, who gave me the look she gives when we're supposed to just go with it. Like, who knew if she'd ever be able to move out of there?

"And what about Dad?" I asked.

"Dad sat right there," she said, pointing to where Nina was sitting, "and just cried." I kept holding on to her. I had never in my entire life held on to my mom like that, in a way where I needed her as much as she needed me.

Having Some Tea

New lemony smell, new floor creaks, new wind outside ruffling the shrubs against my new bedroom window. I'd been living in this room for two months, but now that I knew it was officially mine, everything felt new again. I went downstairs and quietly made myself a mug of apple-cinnamon tea.

Just like in the other house, Auntie Gina had keys set up by the front door, but instead of being in a random dish, they were dangling from these rainbow hooks attached to the wall. She'd made a set for me and a set for Nina, and she put on key chains with our names. I was officially a member of this house. It partly made me have a pang of missing my dad and partly made me so excited I didn't know what to do with myself.

I went and snuggled on the couch and stared out the skylight. It was that sweet moment, right before dawn, when the birds and sun are still too shy to come out.

Then Nina came down, joining me on the couch in her sweats and T-shirt.

"I read all your letters," she said.

"Thanks for writing me one," I said.

"Thanks for telling me all the stuff you heard in the basement."

I sipped my tea.

"You are sneaky, Steffany Sandolini. I gotta give you more credit."

We both kind of giggled.

A sliver of sun peeked between the blinds and swelled. Nina scooted over so close to me I had to steady the mug.

"Steffy," she said. "Remember when Mom said that her dad was mad at her? When you brought her cream puffs?"

I nodded, the weight of the memory giving me an ache.

"I didn't think that was a bad thing," she said. "I think because . . . even if it's a sad memory or something, it's okay. She still remembered something."

Nina had the envelope that Dad had left her the day before the wedding, the day I gave him the picture of Mom. She opened the triangle part and slid out the card. It had a picture of a shiny trumpet on it.

"'Dear Nina,'" she read. "'Keep dancing.'"

We both just sat there, and the air was thick with things we didn't say.

"Are you gonna go back down there," she asked, "to the basement?"

"I don't know," I said. "Maybe."

"Yeah," said Nina.

I didn't think I wanted to know anymore, like I thought I did at first. Maybe grown-ups were right to try to keep secrets, like Carol telling us it was choir practice and all. Maybe it was better to not know the truth. The only problem was that we saw the stashes in the fridge and we saw the bloody knuckles and we saw the empty chair. So we knew. We knew everything.

But maybe it was like if you heard it officially, like I did at those meetings, then that meant there was no hope of something better. And maybe I wasn't ready to give up on the idea of something better.

Bread Crumbs

Everyone was up early in this house. Auntie Gina had cappuccinos and sweet cream ready when we got downstairs. At the end of the counter, there was already a big ball of dough cleeshing under a glass bowl. I didn't know what kind of pasta we were making for later, but I couldn't wait to find out.

Auntie Gina was cracking eggs into another bowl for an omelet. Nina sat at the bar, yawning. I started chopping up yellow peppers and already-cooked chicken sausages, and Harry made toast. In a minute, Auntie Gina tapped me, and I turned around.

"Wire whisk," she said as she traded me the whisk for

the knife and went to cut my peppers and chicken. Giggling, I went to whisk the eggs. It made me think of my mom, of course, but it didn't pull me down. After everything that happened this year, there was something buoying those thoughts that wasn't there before.

We were talking about the wedding and then about Nina's recital coming up, how we were all driving to Charlotte together, and then Harry said he was going to paint the wall in the backyard this summer and did we want to help, and we said yes.

It was a buzzy morning, so different from mornings with Dad and his newspaper. Truth was, I loved both kinds of mornings.

We made an everything omelet, kind of a Kitchen Sink omelet. You basically went into the fridge and took out anything that would taste remotely good with eggs. Could be mushrooms, onions, sausage, shredded cheese, ham, peppers, whatever. Once it was all chopped up, you threw that stuff and whisked eggs in a pan to fry up with some olive oil, salt, and pepper. We had ours with toast and potatoes.

Harry was asking me and Nina all about the move and if we liked our rooms and what we needed, and we said everything was good and thank you.

"So, listen," he said. "I don't want to say too much here, and I won't talk about this again unless you guys want to. But any time you feel like you want to see your dad, it's okay with us. Also, I don't want you to think you ever need to . . . Well, just always call me Harry, okay?"

Nina said okay and I nodded, and I was glad we were eating because I had something to do with my face besides cry. Nobody said anything about how with Dad, you didn't really have a choice about seeing him. He was either around or not, his choice. I guessed it'd just always be like that. Maybe.

They insisted on cleaning up and sent us up to our new rooms, where we got busy. I taped up a picture of me and Dad and Nina eating ice cream at Uncle Louie's. Next to that I put one of me and Mom and Nina and Jean and Helen at the Place. I decorated the walls with these giant orange flowery stickers and put some stuff in my drawers. I framed the dollar that Great-Aunt Lucy had given me, and it hung over my bed. In the bathroom, I put the new hairbrushes that I got us.

My summer was stretching out in front of me. More time in the fancy kitchen, experimenting with the fizzy-water thing and soda maker, biking around the new neighborhood, my cooking classes at Elon that I won, a visit to Charlotte for the recital. Going to Grasshoppers games with Lisa.

I set out a big framed picture of us at the wedding. Nina with her hair up on top of her head, her muscly arms dangling at her sides, her face painted all womany. Or was that an actual woman in there and not just the makeup doing it? My sister's beauty hid underneath me being scared of her sometimes, but in the picture there it was, all glamorous and perfect.

And there were Harry and Auntie Gina with their arms around each other, their eyes reaching out to me with the excitement of their day. And me by my sister, lots going on under my smile, mostly wanting to know what was coming next.

My family.

But my mom would always be my family, and my dad would always be my family. And there was Jean Sawyer, too.

My family was spread all over the place like bread crumbs, and sometimes I didn't know where it was all leading. But it was like Kitchen Sink, where you started out with a batch of stuff, and an idea, and then what you came up with at the end was a completely different flavor. It could still be delicious.

Kitchen Sink Cookbook: A Year in Recipes

An Autobiography by Steffany Falcon Sandolini

Dear Steffany,

I hope this isn't wrong, but I am writing this the day before it's due. Honestly, Mrs. Ashton (I am saying that to you directly, even though it's supposed to be a letter to me about me—but technically you're reading it right now, right?), honestly, I made notes like you suggested. I outlined. I wrote down stories about what people told me I did when I was little and memories that I thought I had. But on this night, the day before this is due, everything's different.

I've been kind of studying my mom's old *Better Homes and Gardens* cookbook from before she got into a car accident. Before she kind of had to stop being a mom who took care of us. I've been kind of studying not the ones that are printed in the book that everyone in the world could look at who has this cookbook, but her own special ones that she thought to tear out of the *Greensboro Daily News* or a magazine, or write down on a scrap of paper, or ask for someone to give to her. Those ones. There are a total of 77 of them spilling out from under the front cover of the cookbook.

What I liked doing when I was studying them was holding them between my fingers and reading them and rereading them. What I liked about it was that I imagined my mom writing the recipe down, and I imagined her planning to make it. I wondered what the occasion was. Was there an occasion? Was it just because it sounded good? I wondered if she had made those recipes for my dad and which ones he liked best. On a wrinkled piece of paper bag there was a scribbled one with no title that had a bay leaf, pineapple, and other stuff. There were lots of brownie recipes in my mom's cursive. An icing recipe written in shakier cursive than my mom's (maybe my grandmother's) on a tiny envelope like the ones that you get in the valentines-for-your-class package.

What I also liked was looking at the dates on some

of them. Most of the ones she cut out from the newspaper had dates on them. I got shivers when there was a date that was a few months before I was born or before my sister, Nina, was born. I saw my mom, sitting there with my dad, dreaming up a good meal, thinking about when she'd make it, feeling us rumbling around in her stomach.

What I didn't know would happen was that I was scared of those dates because they meant that it was before she got hurt. I was scared of those dates because it was when we didn't know that something bad was going to happen. I don't let myself think about her accident too much or about riding in cars. About how if she was in pain and how bad it was and about how she almost died. About how my dad had to leave because of being scared, and he couldn't even really be there to be our dad anymore. I don't let myself think about that too much, and for the first time in my entire life, I am telling myself that's okay. And it's okay to sometimes get bored when we visit her.

What I'm going to do is keep making these recipes for my mom and bringing them to her each time we visit, and in 77 weeks (well, 73, because I've already brought her 4 recipes so far) maybe she will remember something. Maybe she has been remembering all along.

I figured out this year that sometimes people want to be found and sometimes people don't. My dad doesn't (yet). My mom does.

Because of all the things that have happened with my dad this year, I have decided something. I decided that my autobiography is going to be the past year—the most important year of my life—in food. It will be a cookbook so that people will get to know me and remember me the way I know my mom, through my mom's cookbook. Here are all the recipes I made this year:

Banana Bread

* 1¼ cups flour
* 1 teaspoon baking soda
* ¼ teaspoon salt
* ½ teaspoon cinnamon
* 1 cup sugar
* 1 teaspoon vanilla
* 2 eggs
* ½ cup oil
* 3 overripe bananas (brown ones)
* ½ cup chopped walnuts, pecans, or chocolate chips (if you want)

1. Preheat oven to 375 degrees.
2. Put all dry ingredients together and stir.
3. Then put all wet ingredients together and blend.
4. Pour dry ingredients into wet and mix well.
5. Add chopped nuts or chocolate chips.
6. Pour batter into greased 9 x 5-inch pan and bake for 60 minutes at 375 degrees.

Grandpa Falcon's Brussels Sprouts and Egg Whites

* 4–5 egg whites
* 2 cups chopped Brussels sprouts
* ¼ cup chopped scallions
* salt and pepper
* splash milk
* pat butter or margarine

1. Whisk together egg whites, chopped Brussels sprouts, and scallions.
2. Shake on some salt and pepper, and add milk for creaminess.
3. Melt butter in frying pan for a minute over medium heat and then add egg mixture.
4. After a few minutes of stirring, it'll get fluffy and then it's done.
5. Serve with toast and coffee.

Lunch Counter–Style Tuna Melts

* 1 large can tuna, drained (chunk white in water)
* 2 spoonfuls mayonnaise
* dash salt and pepper
* chopped-up pickle
* bread
* Cheddar cheese slices

1. Take out tuna and mix with mayonnaise, salt, pepper, and pickle in bowl.
2. Turn oven on to broil. Put bread on tinfoil and then scoop tuna mixture onto it.
3. Cover tuna with cheese slices. Add another slice of bread on top.
4. Cook in broiler for a few minutes.
5. It'll look like regular toast on top—that's when you know it's done.

Spooky Jell-O

1. Basically, get package of orange Jell-O.
2. Follow directions on package.
3. Put it in the fridge for about an hour.
4. Take it out. Dump a bunch of gummy worms and spiders in it.
5. Pop it back into the fridge for a few hours.

Chicken and Waffles

Fried Chicken:

* 1½ pounds chicken breasts
* 2 eggs, blended
* splash of milk
* couple cups bread crumbs
* garlic salt
* parsley
* butter or margarine

1. Wash all your chicken.
2. Put eggs and milk together in flat dish.
3. Mix bread crumbs and seasonings in separate bowl.
4. Grease up frying pan and set stove to medium heat.
5. Wet each chicken breast in egg mixture, then roll it all over in bread crumbs.
6. Put breasts in pan.
7. Let cook for about 8 minutes on each side, or until breasts are cooked in middle.

Waffles:

* 1 cup flour
* ½ teaspoon baking powder
* ¼ teaspoon baking soda
* ¼ teaspoon salt
* 1 cup buttermilk
* 1 egg
* 2 tablespoons cooking oil
* syrup

1. Mix all dry ingredients in bowl.
2. In separate bowl, mix milk, egg, and oil.
3. Add wet ingredients to dry.
4. Pour into hot waffle iron and make as many waffles as batter will let you.
5. Put chicken breasts right on top of waffles, pour syrup all over them, and go to town.

Spicy Nina-ritos

* chopped garlic (a few cloves)
* ¼ cup chopped onion
* splash cooking oil
* 1 pound ground beef or turkey
* ⅓ cup salsa
* salt, cilantro, cumin, paprika
* sour cream
* guacamole
* diced tomatoes
* grated yellow cheese
* extra salsa
* flour tortillas

1. Toss garlic and onion into frying pan on stove.
2. Simmer in cooking oil and then open package of meat and break it up and sprinkle it over top. Mix together with garlic and onion.
3. Once meat is cooked all the way through, take it off heat and strain it to get grease out.
4. Transfer to serving bowl.
5. Pour in salsa and season with salt and cilantro, and if you like it spicy (we do), add cumin and paprika, but watch out. You might want to use lots of sour cream with every bite.

6. If you're more wimpy, don't use paprika or cumin at all. It'll still taste good.
7. Get out yellow grated cheese, guacamole, diced tomatoes, and sour cream and put each topping in a little bowl on the table. For the guacamole, smush a couple avocados, add a packet of avocado seasoning, and stir.
8. If you want, warm the flour tortillas in the microwave before serving them.

Crock-Pot Thanksgiving Dinner

* a turkey (9 pounds or smaller if you can find one—fresh, not frozen)
* ½ cup finely chopped onion
* 2 cups diced celery
* ½ cup butter
* 8 cups bread, cubed and firmly packed
* ½ tablespoon salt
* 1 teaspoon poultry seasoning
* ¼ teaspoon pepper
* 1 cup water
* ½ can turkey stock

1. Wash turkey.
2. Take out gross innards bag.
3. Let turkey dry overnight in the fridge.
4. In the morning, cook onion and celery in butter in frying pan over low heat, stirring until onion is tender.
5. In large bowl, blend bread cubes and seasonings.
6. Add celery and onion to bread.
7. Toss lightly to blend.
8. Pour water gradually over mixture.

9. Put turkey in Crock-Pot and then stuff stuffing into turkey.
10. Pour turkey stock all over.
11. Put lid on and check your Crock-Pot settings. Cook for the equivalent of 4–5 normal, in the-regular-oven hours. (In our Crock-Pot that would be 6–8 hours on "Auto.")

Safety note: when cooking stuffing inside the turkey, make sure the turkey reaches an internal temperature of 165 degrees Fahrenheit. Use a food thermometer to check. For more safety tips about cooking turkey, check out www.cdc.gov/features/turkeytime.

Day-after-Thanksgiving Kitchen Sink

* ½ cup sliced green peppers
* ½ cup sliced mushrooms
* 1 tablespoon butter
* garlic salt
* 2 cups bits of cooked turkey meat
* 8-ounce can tomato sauce
* 6-ounce can tomato paste
* eggs
* lettuce leaves
* 2 cups cooked rice

1. Fry peppers and mushrooms in frying pan in butter.
2. Season with garlic salt.
3. Add turkey meat and pour tomato sauce and paste over if you want. (When I made this it turned out gross, but maybe you'll have better luck than me.)
4. In another pan, scramble some eggs (about 3).

5. Dump egg mixture into vegetable pan and let cleesh (allow all the ingredients to blend together into one thing).
6. Serve on lettuce leaves as burritos with cooked rice.

Chicken Parmesan

* precooked breaded chicken breasts
* 12-ounce jar pasta sauce
* mozzarella and Parmesan cheeses

1. Put sauce all over chicken, then put cheeses on top of sauce.
2. Bake in oven at around 375 degrees for about 15 minutes. Test chicken for doneness. (It's fully cooked already, but check it anyway.)

Caramel Corn

* 4 bags microwave popcorn
* 1 stick butter or margarine
* ¾ cup brown sugar
* ½ cup light Karo syrup
* 1 teaspoon vanilla
* 1 cup salted, diced pecans

1. Pop corn and set aside.
2. Melt butter.
3. Add brown sugar while butter is still medium hot, then add Karo syrup.
4. Add vanilla and stir.
5. Stir and stir and then stir again.
6. Keep stirring.
7. It shouldn't boil, but it should be hot, and you should keep stirring.
8. Once it starts to thicken, pour in pecans and stir for about another minute or two. You'll know when it's thickened enough. You'll just feel it.

9. Take it off stove and scoop it right onto popcorn.
10. Mix it all together but be careful. You don't want to break some of the popcorns like I did. Refrigerate overnight.

Sausage-and-Pepper Rolls

* 6 sweet or spicy (or a few of both) Italian sausages
* 1–2 capfuls olive oil
* pizza dough
* sliced green peppers
* butter (if you want)

1. Fry up sausages in olive oil over medium heat.
2. Drain grease after they're fully cooked. Set them aside.
3. Roll out pizza dough and cut into pieces.
4. Put sausage and peppers onto dough and then roll like burritos.
5. Press dough back together to seal it up so you can't see the sausage.
6. Bake rolls at 375 degrees for about 8 minutes.
7. Turn over and bake on other side for about 5–8 more minutes.
8. If you want, spread a little butter over rolls right when you take them out.

Gnocchi

* 3–4 medium-sized potatoes
* 10 cups water for the potatoes
* 2 tablespoons butter or margarine
* ½ cup milk
* dash salt
* 5 cups flour
* 3 eggs
* 1 capful olive oil
* extra flour
* 10 quarts water for the pasta
* grated parmesan or Romano cheese

1. Boil potatoes until soft. Peel off skins.
2. Use fork or blender on high speed to mash potatoes. Add butter and milk while you're mashing. Sprinkle on salt.
3. Add mashed potatoes to flour. Mix with wooden spoon until it's evened out into thick crumbs. Add eggs. Mix more with spoon.
4. Then get flour on your hands and knead. Just knead it and knead it and knead it for about 15 or 20 minutes until it's a pretty much kept-together ball.

5. Pour olive oil into the palm of your hand (like lotion) and rub over dough.
6. Sprinkle some flour on table, then put dough on top. Then cover with big bowl for 30 minutes to cleesh.
7. Lift bowl and cut off slab of dough. Flour up your rolling pin and roll it out about ¼ inch thick.
8. Cut that slab into about ½-inch-sized strips.
9. Cut strips into small pieces.
10. Schweet each piece (stick your finger in it, making a little dent). Set aside in big area with flour sprinkled under and on top of gnocchi.
11. When it's all cut, boil big pot of water and add dash salt.
12. Boil gnocchi for about 6–8 minutes but test before turning off water.
13. Rinse gnocchi in colander.
14. Top with sauce (see page 296) and cheese. Mmmmm.

Polenta

* 5 cups water
* 1 cup cornmeal
* dash salt

1. Add salt to water in a large pot and bring to a boil.
2. Pour in cornmeal.
3. Keep stirring and stirring and take off heat once it's creamy paste and not too hard.
4. Serve with pasta sauce and meat or with vegetables.

Blasting NASA Cupcakes

* 1 package chocolate cake mix
* 1 container chocolate frosting

1. Bake cupcakes according to recipe on box.
2. Eat or cut hole out of bottom of each one.
3. Fill hole with frosting.
4. Try and smush cakey cupcake around gooey frosting.
5. Then freeze. Enjoy them while orbiting galaxy!

Yam-Pecan Pie

Crust:

* ice-cold water
* 1 cup flour
* ½ teaspoon baking soda
* ¼ teaspoon salt
* ⅓ cup plus 1 tablespoon shortening

1. Put cup of water in freezer.
2. Then combine flour, baking soda, and salt.
3. Now add shortening (be ready to use lots of paper towels when you're washing up, because water won't cut it).
4. When mixture's kind of still powdery but a little sticky, get cup of water out of freezer and put in 3 tablespoons from it. Ice-ice-cold is best.
5. Now stir. It should start to resemble dough.
6. Knead for a while into ball.
7. Put it on top of sheet of waxed paper. Then put another piece of waxed paper on top of that.

8. Roll it out as flat as you can get it without it ripping.
9. Peel off from waxed paper and press into pie tin.
10. With fork, poke light holes around middle and sides.
11. Pull off excess dough around rim of tin and save it in fridge or freezer. Put crust in fridge as well to wait for filling to be done.

Pie Filling:

* 1 cup mashed-up yams (about 2 medium-sized ones or 1 giant, enormous one)
* ⅓ cup brown sugar
* ¼ teaspoon cinnamon
* ¾ teaspoon ginger
* ¾ cup boiling hot milk
* dash salt
* 2 beaten eggs

1. Preheat oven to 375 degrees.
2. Add yams to brown sugar, cinnamon, ginger, hot milk, salt, and eggs.

3. Stir this up good, let it cool, and then pour into crust.
4. Bake for 20 minutes.
5. While that's in oven, get started on crumble topping.
6. After pie cooks for 20 minutes, take it out and sprinkle crumble topping on top and then cook for another 25 minutes.
7. Put giant blob of whipped cream on top and be prepared to pass out from joy.

Crumble Topping:

- half stick soft butter or margarine
- ½ cup brown sugar
- ¾ cup chopped pecans
- whipped cream

Put butter, brown sugar, and pecans together and stir them around until they're combined.

Pie-Crust Cinnamon Rolls:

1. Take leftover pie-crust dough, or you could use something like leftover lemon bar crust dough, and pull off little balls of it.
2. Roll them out into these little snakelike strips.
3. Sprinkle them with cinnamon and sugar.
4. Roll them up like snails and put them on cookie sheet or pie tin.
5. Pop them in oven at 400 degrees for about 6–8 minutes, or until bottoms are light brown. (Your kitchen will smell like the food court at the mall.)

Pizza Frittas

* 4–5 tablespoons cooking oil
* pizza dough
* powdered sugar

1. Fill pan with cooking oil and turn on stove to medium heat. (If you have a deep fryer, use that. We don't. A regular old frying pan is good, too.)
2. Grab off hunks of pizza dough and make them into doughnut shapes.
3. Put them on the sizzling oil.
4. Cook on both sides until light brown. (Watch for flying grease.)
5. Put on plate and dab off extra grease with paper towel.
6. Sprinkle with powdered sugar. You just made Italian doughnuts!

Cream Puffs

* 1 cup water
* stick butter or margarine
* ⅛ teaspoon salt
* 1 cup flour
* 4 eggs
* whipped cream

1. Boil water, butter, and salt.
2. Then add flour and stir real good. It'll turn into this sticky ball after a little while.
3. Take it off the burner and let it cool.
4. Preheat oven to 400 degrees right about now.
5. Add eggs to mixture, stirring each one in.
6. Scoop 12 blops onto greased cookie sheet and bake for 30–35 minutes.
7. When they are lightly browned but not crispy—they should stay soft—take them out and let them cool.
8. Slice them in half parallel to the table and load them up with whipped cream filling, like sandwiches. Some people use ice cream, or you could actually put anything you want in there, like chicken salad if you're going

that route, or Nutella. Anyway, we always do whipped cream, and we always end up squirting some into our mouths straight from the can.

Smoothies

* 1 cup fresh or frozen fruit (I used strawberries)
* splashes of milk or apple juice
* 6-ounce thing of yogurt (I always use vanilla, but you can use plain or Greek or with fruit or whatever kind you like best)
* crushed ice

1. Put everything in blender.
2. Turn on Puree for as long as it takes for it to look like a milk shake.
3. Turn off blender and pour in more milk or juice if you need to and then blend again.
4. Serve in fancy smoothie cups.

Jeannie Beannie's Lemon Bars

* ½ stick butter
* 2 tablespoons powdered sugar
* ½ cup flour
* 1 egg
* ½ cup sugar
* 2 tablespoons lemon juice
* 1 tablespoon flour
* ⅛ teaspoon baking powder
* extra powdered sugar (for sprinkling)

Lemon bar crust:

1. Preheat oven to 325 degrees.
2. In small mixing bowl, cream butter and powdered sugar and then gradually beat in flour.
3. Press into bottom of ungreased 9 x 9 x 2 pan.
4. Bake for about 8 minutes, or until edges are lightly browned.

Filling:

1. Beat egg, sugar, lemon juice, flour, and baking powder.
2. Mix until frothy and then pour over warm crust.
3. Bake at 375 degrees for 12 minutes, or until lightly browned.
4. Sprinkle top with powdered sugar.

Anytime Fancy Layer Cake

Chocolate Layer:

* ¾ cup unsweetened cocoa powder
* 2 cups flour
* 2 teaspoons baking soda
* 1½ teaspoons baking powder
* ¼ teaspoon salt
* ¾ cup butter or margarine (softened)
* 2 cups sugar
* 3 eggs
* 1⅓ cups milk

1. Preheat oven to 350 degrees.
2. Put all dry ingredients together and mix.
3. Put wet ingredients in separate bowl, except for milk.
4. Add wet and dry ingredients together gradually. Just a little bit of wet to dry, then blend for a while. Then a little bit, then blend. More. Blend.
5. When it's all together except milk, add milk gradually.
6. Bake for 35–40 minutes in one big 9 x 11-inch pan or in two smaller 8-inch-square or round pans (for a double layer).

Vanilla Layer:

* 2½ cups flour
* 2½ teaspoons baking powder
* ½ teaspoon salt
* ¾ cup soft butter or margarine
* 1¾ cups sugar
* 3 eggs
* 2 teaspoons vanilla
* 1¼ cups milk

1. Preheat oven to 375 degrees.
2. Stir together flour, baking powder, and salt.
3. In a big bowl, beat butter on high until it's like thick pudding.
4. Gradually add sugar to butter until it's all mixed together.
5. Add eggs and beat more after each one.
6. Beat in vanilla.
7. Add in a little of the flour mixture, then beat.
8. Add in a little of the milk, then beat.
9. Keep alternating like that until every ingredient is in.

10. Bake at 375 degrees in a 9 x 11-inch pan for 20–25 minutes, or in two 8-inch square or round pans for 30–35 minutes.

Carrot Layer:

- 2 cups carrot strings (about two whole carrots' worth—peel your carrots first, then shred them using a grater or the peeler)
- 2 eggs
- 1 cup sugar
- 1 cup brown sugar
- 1 cup cooking oil
- 2 tablespoons vanilla
- 2½ cups flour
- 2 teaspoons baking soda
- ½ teaspoon cinnamon
- ¼ teaspoon salt

1. Preheat oven to 350 degrees.
2. Beat carrot peelings with eggs, sugar, brown sugar, cooking oil, and vanilla. Set aside.
3. In another bowl, dump in flour, baking soda, cinnamon, and salt and stir.

4. Mix wet with dry ingredients.
5. Pour into a 9 x 11-inch pan or two 8-inch square or round pans and bake 30 minutes.

Grandma Sandolini's S's and O's

* 1 cup pretty warm water
* 2½ teaspoons active dry yeast
* 3 cups flour
* ½ teaspoon salt
* 5 tablespoons cold butter or margarine
* ⅔ cup sugar for rolling cookies
* 1 container white frosting
* red food coloring

1. In small bowl, pour water over yeast and stir until it dissolves yeast. Cover and set aside.
2. Put together flour and salt, then add butter and blend until everything is mixed but still powdery.
3. Add yeast mixture and stir everything together.
4. Put dough into greased bowl, then turn it over so other side gets greased, too.
5. Cover bowl with plastic wrap and wait an hour. When you look at it again, it should have doubled in size!

6. After dough rises, press it down again and put it in fridge for about an hour.
7. Put long sheets waxed paper out on table. Sprinkle some sugar down on waxed paper so dough doesn't stick.
8. Get dough out of fridge and press it down on paper.
9. Cut square of dough into about 7 strips. Cut each strip into 6 pieces (so 42 pieces total).
10. Roll each piece on sugary waxed paper under palms of your hands.
11. Preheat oven to 325 degrees right about now.
12. Make *S* shapes with some of them and *O* shapes with other ones.
13. Put them on ungreased cookie sheet. Let them puff up a little bit before you bake them.
14. Bake about 15 minutes. Turn them over, bake another 10 minutes.
15. Let cool.
16. Then use frosting to glaze half the cookies with white frosting and half with pink frosting. For pink frosting—put half the

white frosting in separate bowl, add a few drops of red food coloring, and stir. My grandma frosted all the S's with pink and all the O's with white, but you can mix them up.

Sesame Nut Candy

* 1 cup toasted sesame seeds (you can buy them at the store already toasted)
* 1 cup roasted unsalted peanuts (same thing)
* ½ cup sugar
* ¼ cup rice syrup
* ¼ teaspoon salt
* 1 teaspoon water
* 2 teaspoons vegetable oil
* ½ cup freeze-dried blueberries

1. Put sesame seeds and peanuts in bowl together.
2. Then put sugar, syrup, salt, and water in pot over low heat.
3. Stir a little while it's getting hot so it doesn't stick to sides.
4. Start stirring when it starts to boil and then don't let it boil too long. Keep stirring, and when it starts to form sugary strands, take it off heat and add sesame seeds and peanuts.
5. Put big clump of stuff on cutting board that you put vegetable oil onto beforehand.

6. Smash down clump until it's kind of flat.
7. Pour on blueberries and roll over whole thing with rolling pin. It's going to start getting hard, so you kind of have to do it fast or ask someone to help smush it down really good.
8. Cut it into squares—it'll be hard, so you might need help using a big knife (I did).

one hundred spaghetti strings

* ⅓ cup onion
* 3–4 cloves garlic
* few capfuls olive oil
* 3 egg whites
* 1 pound ground beef
* 7–8 pieces of bread left out overnight
* pepper
* 1–2 tablespoons salt for meatballs, sauce, dough, and boiling water
* garlic powder
* splash milk
* 6 sweet and/or spicy sausages
* 4 cans (8-ounce) tomato sauce
* 4 cans (6-ounce) tomato paste
* parsley, oregano, and basil
* 7 cups flour
* 4 eggs
* a little extra water, in case dough is stubborn
* 10 quarts water for the pasta
* Parmesan cheese

Meatballs and Sauce:

1. Dice onion, pound garlic. Peel off any leftover skin. Put it all in big cooking pot on stove along with some olive oil. Turn on stove

to medium heat and let onions and garlic cook slowly. While they're cooking, start meatballs.

2. Separate whites from yolks (save yolks in fridge for something else, maybe an omelet or some kind of eggy sauce).
3. Crinkle hard bread into bread crumbs.
4. Squish ground beef around in big mixing bowl.
5. Shake in ½ tsp salt, pepper, garlic powder, and bread crumbs.
6. Pour in milk and egg whites.
7. Clump everything into ball.
8. Roll chunks into small balls. Set balls aside.
9. Breathe in flavor of onions and garlic on stove.
10. Peel off casing of sausages.
11. Break sausage meat on top of onions and garlic. Let brown.
12. Pour in sauce and paste. Then fill each empty can with water and pour that in, too.
13. Sprinkle in parsley, oregano, basil, and ¼ tsp salt.
14. Turn stove to high heat. Boil for 20 minutes.
15. Drop in meatballs.
16. Simmer sauce on low for however many hours you can. Stir occasionally.

Spaghetti:

1. Combine flour, eggs, and 1 tsp salt.
2. Stir dough mixture with wooden spoon. It'll be a little stubborn at first, probably.
3. Fold dough every which way.
4. Press dough into table with your muscles!
5. Knead dough like crazy.
6. Cleesh dough under bowl for 30 minutes.
7. Slice off chunk. Sprinkle with flour.
8. Roll out into thin piece.
9. Cut into long strips.
10. Feed each strip into pasta machine.
11. Fill a giant pot ¾ full of water and set it on to boil. Add dash salt.
12. Put in pasta when water's boiling. Cook for about 8 minutes, stirring occasionally.
13. After pouring into collander and rinsing, serve.
14. Drench with sauce.
15. Sprinkle with cheese.
16. Devour.

Sincerely,

Steffany Falcon Sandolini

One Hundred Thank-Yous

Anyone who writes, or creates anything from scratch, knows about the time invested in putting a project together (for me—years). There were so many details and circumstances that had to come together in order to make this book cleesh.

First, there were my writing groups and "third eye" friends: Julie Stainer, Marcia Lerner, Cathleen Davitt Bell, Shannon Rigney Keane, Jennifer Ostrega Gold, March Schrader, Wendy Herlich, Sasha Domnitz, Mike Gold, and my family—I am beyond grateful for your time spent reading this book when it was scraps in a Word document. Thank you all for your love and encouragement.

There was also research. One of my best friends in the world, Heidi Verhaal Levine, hosted me in Greensboro, and up to the minute before this book went to print she was promptly responding to texts about bus routes and street names. The folks at Betsy's Support Site for Traumatic Brain Injury Recovery and Rehabilitation answered all my questions and continue to provide a wealth of information and links to additional resources for those affected by traumatic brain injuries. Connie Gold educated me on Korean cooking. My amazing Auntie Anna and my mom and dad reminded me of so many of our family's old recipes. And my dear cousin Mary Beth Salardino shared with me her feelings about growing up. Thank you all for letting me in on these details and personal experiences.

Then there was Jocelyn Davies, who I met on a bus when I asked if the aisle seat next to her was free. I didn't know she was an editor. Thank you, Jocelyn, for being easy to talk to and open, from that very first second. Thank you for seeing the potential in this book and for guiding me through the process of making it better. There was Elizabeth Harding, who turned the mysterious world of publishing into something very straightforward and transparent. Thank you for your humor, steadiness, and cupcakes.

And there, always, was my sister, Nancy West, and all my dear friends who continue to make me laugh until I'm crying, who listen, who tell me the truth, and who prop me up when I desperately need propping.

And there, always, were my mom and dad, Frank and

June Nails. Since I was a child, I have watched you struggle through recipes and life in order to put together something amazing. I continue to observe your every move, hang on your every word, and learn by your example. I haven't yet found the words to best express my infinite gratitude and love for you both.

And not always, but since 2007 and then 2012, there have been Zac and Simon, the two key ingredients that made me for the first time understand the power of tradition, that showed me how important it is to know who you are and where you came from. I love you, my dear sons.

Finally, I am grateful to all of the chefs from the extended Nails and Lanza families for every hot meal that you put on the table after an exhausting day in the steel mill, on the farm, in the coal mine, on the football field, in the classroom, and in the home rearing children.

And reader, one hundred thank-yous to you, for picking up this book. I hope that the next meal you share with your family or friends is full of love.